A DARK VAMPIRE CURSE

NIKKI ST. CROWE

BLACKWELL HOUSE

NEWSLETTER

Want exclusive access to bonus content and news about upcoming books? Sign-up for Nikki's newsletter to stay in the loop!

https://www.subscribepage.com/nikkistcrowe

CONTENT WARNING

CHAPTER 1

EMERY

Emery Blake could read minds. And in all twenty-five years of her life, she had yet to figure out a way to shut it off. Which made just about every relationship a minefield.

As her boss sped through the next intersection, she tried to focus on anything other than hearing his inner thoughts.

Tanner Bernard Jenison III was just two years older than she was, but he was in charge of a multi-million-dollar development company despite the fact that he didn't know much about how to run it.

Emery was his assistant, and while Tanner was the type of guy to think *assistant* was synonymous with *disposable underwear*, he knew she had a knack for reading people.

She could only imagine what he'd do if he found out the talent was *literal* and not figurative.

Oh the secrets she had of his. She could make a fortune selling them. And then she could get out of the dingy apartment she shared with her cousin, who slept till noon and shuffled through boyfriends like a deck of cards.

Except Emery wasn't an asshole, and her moral compass knew true north.

Instead, she was stuck working for Tanner, kissing his butt, cleaning up his messes, and pretending she couldn't hear all of his slimy thoughts.

She was *this close* to a promotion. Tanner had been thinking about it just three months ago. Granted, he was drinking wine that night, and Wine Tanner was a sentimental one, but if he thought it then, surely he was capable of thinking it *now*.

If Emery could seal this deal tonight with Rhys Roman, the mysterious, extremely powerful billionaire then she could—

Emery sure has let herself go.

Fucking hell, Tanner!

He popped a mint into his mouth, face blank.

What kind of girl does Rhys Roman like anyway? Maybe I should've told Em to wear something slutty. No, bad form, dude. You can't tell your secretary to dress slutty for a business deal.

Secretary? Her official title was Executive Assistant.

Emery cleared her throat loudly hoping to distract Tanner, but it was useless.

Em used to be hot. I guess Michael really did fuck her up. Girl gets dumped, and suddenly, her life is over.

Emery turned to the car's passenger window and gritted her teeth.

What Tanner thought didn't matter.

And yeah, maybe she had eaten a few too many batches of chocolate chip cookies since the breakup. And maybe she had grown a little too fond of Twizzlers and red wine. And yeah, she did order out almost every night because who had time to cook when your life was falling apart?

Goddamn Michael anyway.

They'd been together nearly five years when he broke things off.

Michael was the only exception to the whole mental-minefield. When they first met, his thoughts were distant and warm. He always had a kind thing to think about her. And when he wasn't thinking about Emery, he was brainstorming ways to solve the problem of the world's overuse of plastic.

As a lead scientist at an up-and-coming renewable resource company, he spent hours just thinking about plastic bottles and bags.

Over the years, his thoughts became a pleasant background noise until Emery stopped hearing them entirely. It was such a relief. So easy to be herself around him when she wasn't constantly lingering on his thoughts, looking for those mines.

And then one night, he caught her off guard while they watched an episode of Emery's favorite historical drama. It was about the fourth time she watched it, and maybe the second for Michael.

His thoughts wandered.

When should I tell her?

Tell her what? She kept her gaze on the TV and tried to *la-la-la* her way through whatever he was puzzling over.

But as usual, her curiosity got the better of her.

I can't do this for much longer.

Oh shit.

I should just tell her now. I should tell her it's not working for me anymore and that I'm leaving.

In that moment, Emery literally thought her heart was breaking. Like actually cracking down the center and crumbling to pieces.

What a horrible feeling it was to think your life was all

sunshine and roses only to find out it was careening over the edge of a cliff. And worse, you couldn't do anything about it.

Emery couldn't tell Michael she'd heard his thoughts.

She couldn't ask him where they'd gone wrong and what she could do to fix it.

For the next three weeks, she turned herself into a pretzel, trying to be the perfect girlfriend. She didn't complain. She didn't nag. She made herself small, but attentive, calm, and giving. She initiated sex around every corner.

And then, she spent most nights in the bathroom, throwing up, because she was such a ball of nerves.

But none of it mattered.

When Michael finally summoned enough courage to tell her, all of her objections dried up on the tip of her tongue. Like cotton candy, there one minute, gone the next.

Michael moved out of the apartment a week later, and Emery looked around at all the empty spaces on the shelves and just sobbed. She was going to be alone for the rest of her damn life. Cursed to hear the intimate details of everyone's overstuffed headspace.

She seriously considered buying a cabin in the woods and never leaving it.

Could life be any crueler?

Oh sure, of course it could. Because it turned out Emery couldn't afford a nice two-bedroom apartment in Welsh District on just her salary. And with the rental market in Saint Sabine at an all-time high, beggars certainly couldn't be choosers.

Which was why she was now subletting a room from her cousin in a dingy apartment in the Industrial Park.

Every morning when she woke up to the sound of a train blasting by, she had to remind herself she was lucky to have a roof over her head. But gods, she wanted more. She wanted to escape the life she was stuck in.

Next to her, Tanner downshifted as the street spilled downhill into the part of the city known as the Second Quarter. The street curved around the east side of Garden Park before turning back again. In the distance, moonlight glittered on the dark waters of Chantilly Harbor.

Emery loved this part of the city. Sometimes she fantasized about what it'd be like to rent one of the lofts in the upstairs of one of the old century buildings. The kind of place that still had the original tin ceilings and leaded glass windows and mottled brick walls.

But the Second was one of the most expensive neighborhoods in Saint Sabine, and even with a raise, it'd be unlikely she could afford it.

Dreams would have to stay dreams. Unless a goddamn miracle happened.

Tanner stopped at a red light. The little sports car idled loudly. He stole a glance at Emery out of the corner of his eye and said, "You got that game face ready?"

"I was born with my game face on."

He laughed and shook his head.

Emery readjusted her skirt, tugging it further down her thighs. Tanner thought the outfit wasn't slutty, but it was the shortest skirt she owned. When he told her about this mission tonight, he *had* given her some fashion advice, though clearly not the kind he'd wanted to give.

"Wear something sexy, but professional," he'd said. "Think Angelina Jolie meets Michelle Obama."

You couldn't mash up Angelina and Michelle! They were their own fierce women.

Emery did the best with what she had to work with and paired the short black skirt with the only high-end shirt she owned. It was a sleeveless plain white cotton, but buttery soft. To round out the outfit, she'd wore her stilettos and hoop earrings.

Using some advice from her best friend Morgan, she'd done a smoky eye, using the makeup set Morgan bought her for her last birthday.

Emery thought she looked fucking fierce.

Tanner thought she looked puffy and sad.

If she murdered him, could she get away with it?

Not for the first time, she wished her abilities went both ways. If she could just plant a thought or two into Tanner's head...

But what would she try to get out of him?

What she wanted was respect, and while Tanner had his shining moments, respect didn't appear to be in his wheelhouse.

When the traffic light changed, Tanner hit the gas, and the speedy sports car darted through the intersection. Emery clutched at the door handle. She had been on dozens of business meetings with Tanner, but he'd never been this amped up.

Of course this wasn't like those other meetings.

And Rhys Roman wasn't just any businessman.

And technically, they didn't even have a meeting. Tanner got word from one of his friends that Mr. Roman had been spotted at Club Shade earlier in the night.

Tanner was hoping to "run into him". And then they were winging it.

It wasn't the way Emery liked to conduct business, but Tanner had been vying for Mr. Roman's attention for months. If she didn't know any better, she'd think Tanner was a Rhys Roman fangirl.

Within minutes, they were parked in the lot next to Club

Shade. Emery hurried out ahead of Tanner, and the humid summer air hit her like a wet blanket.

Please let there be air conditioning in this club.

There were seven original districts of Saint Sabine that dated all the way back to the late 1700s. The Second District was a mix of super old saltbox buildings, 18th century warehouses, and early 1900s art deco buildings.

Whoever was on the council for Second District made it a point to protect the historical buildings. There weren't many left in Saint Sabine. But old buildings also meant it was harder to get air conditioning.

"I hate the Second," Tanner mused as they came around to the street front. "It stinks like fish and old leather."

Emery breathed in. She could definitely smell the fish, but it was faint and far away. The fishing docks were a good two miles southeast from Club Shade. Across the street, a band played a jazzy tune on the corner outside of Glady's, their music bouncing off the surrounding buildings. String lights had been hung from the second story wrought iron balconies and wove in and out of overflowing flower boxes. The air was perfumed with the scent of flowers and street food.

How could anyone hate the Second? It was so vibrant and beautiful and full of magic.

Emery would literally give a kidney to live in the Second.

"Come on," Tanner said and ushered her toward the large double doors of Club Shade. The pulsing beat of pop music filtered out into the street. A muscle-bound guy in a black t-shirt opened the door for them, and it creaked on its hinges.

Tanner ran his hand through his hair and gave himself a silent pep talk as they entered.

You're a shark. A tiger shark. No, a hammerhead shark. This deal is meant to be yours.

He smiled over at Emery. She smiled back.

"After you," he said.

The entrance was dimly lit, and fire danced in glass orbs that hung from the ceilings. How the hell did they get that kind of thing to pass building inspections? Something like that could easily start a fire.

People lingered in the lobby, some embraced in heavy make out sessions.

When a girl caught Emery blatantly staring, she smirked and waggled her finger for Emery to join.

"Oh, no, thanks," she said and hurried away, feeling the blush rise in her face.

The lobby ended at a stone archway that led to an iron staircase. The music was so loud, it rattled in Emery's bones. The heady smell of writhing bodies permeated the air.

Tanner pushed past her and started down the iron stairs. Emery trailed her hand along the banister to keep her balance as she descended. Maybe stilettos weren't a smart pick considering the stairs were open-grate metal and every other step, the heel of her shoe went straight through.

When they reached the lower level, Emery gave herself a silent congratulatory high-five for not careening to her death.

She came up behind Tanner as he scanned the crowd in the swirling lights of the club.

The good thing about collective partying was that most people were either drunk or high, and intoxicated minds didn't think as much as sober ones.

It gave Emery room to breathe. Which was a good thing.

She had to save all of her focus and mojo for Rhys Roman.

Now, where was the mysterious billionaire?

CHAPTER 2

RHYS

THERE WAS A TIME WHEN RHYS COULD CONTROL THE URGE TO rip out a throat with his bare teeth.

That was before the curse.

The bloodlust pounding in his head somehow followed the exact beat of the techno music pulsing through the sound system of Club Shade. He was surrounded by dancing mortal bodies in the flickering lights of the club, and the line between his sanity and predatory instinct was growing fucking thin.

It would take him less than ten minutes to drain every single human here.

He was ancient, and they were insignificant, and he was losing his fucking grip.

"Rhys." Dane came around the private booth in the back of Club Shade, a pinch of annoyance between his dark brows.

Dane was Rhys's second-in-command. He wasn't one of Rhys's Turned, but Rhys trusted him like he was. He had showed more loyalty than Ramses, who was Rhys's first Turned vampire and currently MIA, the bastard.

"What is it?" Rhys bit out.

Dane nabbed one of the whisky shots from the table and slung it back. The table was littered with empty glasses and at least a dozen full ones. Sometimes alcohol dulled the bloodlust. Sometimes it didn't.

A trio of girls sauntered over and lingered purposefully in Rhys's line of sight.

One of them whispered into the ear of the other, "I heard fucking Rhys Roman is as close to fucking a god as you can get."

The third girl, bolder than the others, stepped closer. She was wearing a fishnet shirt over a lacey black bra and a skirt so short, it might as well have been panties. Glitter shimmered along her temples and along her clavicle.

She was dressed to attract attention, but Rhys's gaze sunk to the pretty blue vein pulsing in her throat.

"Care for some company?" she purred.

The beat of music faded away. There was only Rhys and the surge of blood in her veins.

As his incisors sharpened to razor-like points, his body went impossibly still, muscles tense, ready to strike.

He could drain all three in less than a minute. Sink his teeth into their flesh and drink them back until the breath stuttered from their throats.

His heart beat harder, thinking about it, about the sweet tang of their blood...

"Little pets," Dane said and ushered them along with the wide span of his arms, "not tonight, I'm afraid."

Rhys blinked and eased back into the booth. He brought his thumb and forefinger to the bridge of his nose as the dull ache of unspent hunger bloomed through his skull.

The girls bemoaned the rejection, but Dane was relentless. It was a characteristic Rhys valued most. Dane always got the job done.

When he came back to the table alone, Dane said, "You good?"

"I'm fine."

There was a growl to the edge of Rhys's words, one he didn't bother hiding.

Rhys wasn't fucking fine.

Dane blew out a breath. "Well, if you're *fine*... I need you in back."

"Why?"

"Cole got into a bit of trouble."

In a blur of movement, Rhys was out of the booth and on his feet. "Where?"

"This way."

They went down the dimly lit hallway that led away from the dance floor back to the VIP rooms. The music faded, but the deep pulse of it still vibrated through the concrete floor. And with Rhys's extra sensory hearing, he could have picked out the beat of the music from a half-mile away.

It was here, once Rhys was out of the swarm of human bodies that he finally picked up the smell of blood. The sweet coppery tang of it overrode the sweat and sharp tinge of alcohol in the air.

How the fuck did he miss it before?

Too caught up in his own bloodlust.

How much longer did they have? If *he* was losing his edge, they might already be on the downward slide.

The witch curse hadn't come with a countdown clock, but Rhys could feel it reaching its end just the same.

Before he was Turned, Rhys had been a prince, the son of a mad king. And now he was about to go mad himself.

How fucking poetic.

Dane pushed through the third door on the left, and Rhys slipped in around him.

Surrounded by carnage and blood, Rhys's eyes shifted. Glowing blue eyes ringed in deepest black. Vampire eyes. The eyes of hunger.

The eyes of a monster.

Thankfully, everyone in the room, save for the vampires, was already dead.

"The fuck did you do?" Rhys scowled at Cole.

The younger vampire was slung haphazardly over a velvet sofa. His shirt was torn, but his skin unmarred. Blood covered him in splatters and smudges. His fangs were still out, but his eyes were heavy and satiated.

Cole laughed. "I got drunk on douchebag blood."

The floor was covered in dead bodies.

Six to be exact.

Mixed with the scent of blood was the stench of cheap body spray.

Rhys stepped over the men and yanked Cole upright by the collar of his shirt. "Tell me what happened."

"Okay. Okay." Cole held up his hands in surrender and Rhys let him go. "We were playing poker, and I caught one of them cheating. It went downhill from there."

"*Downhill* is an understatement," Dane said.

"What else was I supposed to do?"

"Oh I don't know Cole, enthrall them? Make them dance the jig? Leave? It's not as if you need the money."

"It wasn't about the money." Cole grabbed a bottle of Jack from the table and took a long swig. Cards were strewn all over the table and floor.

"I don't really give a fuck what it was about," Rhys said. "Now we have to clean this shit up."

"Mmm," was Cole's reply.

With a growl, Rhys nabbed the bottle from Cole's grip and slung it back. The alcohol burned down his throat, but it wasn't what he wanted and it wasn't what he needed.

How much longer could he keep this shit together?

How long until Cole went on a bender in the middle of a grocery store at dinnertime?

As the alcohol turned cold in his gut, Rhys set the bottle aside and surveyed the mess. He didn't feel like hauling dead bodies right now. He didn't feel like doing anything other than hunting.

"Call Zoz," he said.

The old man was a ghoul who specialized in disposing of bodies and cleaning up the aftermath so it was impossible to detect any misdeeds.

Rhys used him in a pinch.

Dane looked around. "It isn't gonna be cheap."

"I don't care. I don't have fucking time for this." Rhys stepped over a muscle-bound guy wearing a pink tank top and made his way for the door. He had to get out of here before the blood got to him. Before it all got to him.

But as he turned away from the carnage, a figure appeared in front of him, and his finely-tuned instincts immediately engaged.

Rhys crossed the room in a blink and reached out for the uninvited figure only for his hand to go straight *through* it.

It wasn't a *who*, but a *what*.

An Oracle.

The specters appeared out of thin air to issue death omens, dire warnings, and cryptic predictions.

They were controlled by Ciri, Queen of the Oracles, a

woman who was not exactly an ally of Rhys's. Not an enemy either.

"This night just keeps getting better and better," Dane muttered.

Oracles were always young girls, hair as white as the moon with colorless eyes to match. They always wore sheer white capes around white gauzy gowns.

A lot of mortal ghost stories were based on sightings of Oracles. Rhys wasn't entirely sure where they originated—were they ghosts? Or had they once been mortal? Ciri had never been forthcoming with the details.

What Rhys did know was that they didn't smell of this world. It was hard to put into words, exactly, but when an Oracle showed up, the air took on this deep, primordial scent that poked at Rhys's subconscious, the threads of the monster inside of him.

Ramses had a theory that the Oracles came from Alius, another world where all supernatural beings originated.

But Rhys thought that was bullshit.

Alius was a fable, an urban legend.

Ramses was smarter than just about any other person Rhys had ever met, but sometimes, he read *too* much.

Now, when the Oracle spoke, her voice echoed around itself like she was in a cave. "You seek the key to your curse."

"If that's what you've come to tell me, you're wasting your time."

Rhys had been seeking the key to his curse for over two hundred years, and he'd been asking Ciri for help nearly as long. Her response had always been, "You got yourself into this mess. Now get yourself out."

But at this point, she must have known that the longer she held out, the more danger Rhys and his Turned posed to the city. Because the curse effected his entire line. If he went mad, they'd all go mad. And any vampire that lost control was a risk to the entire supernatural community.

It was for precisely that reason why several other vampire houses had made an attempt on his life. Rhys couldn't exactly blame them. He'd have done the same.

Thankfully, he wasn't easy to kill.

The Oracle's cape billowed in a phantom breeze even though the VIP room was shut up tight.

"You'll find the key in two parts," the Oracle went on.

Cole grinned. "Oh, a treasure hunt."

"Shut up," Dane said.

Rhys narrowed his eyes. "Go on."

"The first part," the girl said, "TS Jenison."

Rhys looked at Dane over his shoulder. Dane shrugged.

TS Jension was a development company owned by a daddy's boy.

The fuck did Tanner Jenison have to do with breaking the curse?

And then—*right*.

"It's the building," Rhys said.

TS Jenison, Inc was currently located in a building that had once been owned by the Ravenwood witches. The very same witches that had borne the curse over two centuries before.

The Ravenwoods still resided in the city, but they'd made themselves scarce after Rhys threatened to kill every last one of them. Witches didn't live as long as vampires, and they were a lot easier to kill.

But Rhys suspected the current generation of Ravenwoods didn't exactly know how to undo the curse anyway, so what was the point in rooting them out?

They couldn't help him. And the longer this went on, the more he believed *no one* could.

"What's the second part?" he asked.

The ghostly figure turned away, and the cape billowed out. "The girl."

"The fuck. What girl?" Rhys took a step toward her as if to stop her, but the Oracle disappeared, leaving behind only a shimmering white mist.

Fucking Ciri and her fucking Oracles.

Rhys closed his eyes and ran a hand back through his hair.

"Well, that was helpful," Dane said. "Ciri needs to teach her Oracles better communication skills."

Rhys needed to think. Needed to clear his head.

To Dane and Cole, he said, "Get Zoz on this mess. Have him come through the back door. Then you two come straight home."

Cole rolled his eyes. "I don't need a babysitter or—"

"You will go home," Rhys said. "Or you will be dead by sunrise."

Cole grumbled. "Fine. Buzzkill."

"Where are *you* going?" Dane said to Rhys.

"I'll be home later."

Rhys left the room and shut the door behind him, sealing in the stench of blood and sweat. If only he could shut out the rising tide of bloodlust.

They were running out of time, and he was running thin on control. If he wasn't careful, he might just sink his teeth into the next person he ran into.

CHAPTER 3

EMERY

Come on, Rhys Roman, where are you?

Emery had asked a dozen people if they'd seen Rhys and then read their answering thoughts to no avail. A group of girls said they saw him earlier in the night in one of the private booths in the back of Club Shade, but when Emery finally made her way around the club, the booth was empty.

This guy was like a ghost.

A rich, powerful, ghost that everyone wanted a piece of, and yet, no one seemed capable of pinning down.

It was a challenge Emery really wanted to win. And she was in the unique position to know all of his hidden thoughts, his darkest secrets. She could totally do this.

Rhys Roman would never see her coming.

If only she could find him.

It didn't help that she didn't know exactly what he looked like. There were no pictures of him on the internet. No selfies. No media photos. Not even a business headshot.

She was totally running blind.

"Anything yet?" Tanner asked when he found her later.

"Nothing."

Tanner cursed and scratched at the back of his head. He was desperate to strike a deal with Rhys. Like Emery, he wanted to win the challenge.

If there was one thing every businessman in Saint Sabine coveted above all else, it was making a deal with Mr. Roman. Tanner's desire was part pride, part greed. He wanted to claim the untouched waterfront on the southeast end of the city and build a high-end hotel and luxury condominiums.

The Roman family had owned the land for as long as anyone could remember.

It was the most sought-after stretch on the entire eastern seaboard. Everyone from Saint Sabine to Japan had offered Rhys ungodly amounts of money in order to buy that land and Rhys had said no to every single one.

Tanner was hoping that the man had some other need or want, something he could offer Rhys in exchange for the land, or at least the leasing of it.

That's where Emery came in.

She did a ton of research before this meeting but came up with nothing that would give her an edge. After hours of scouring the Internet, she still only had the surface level facts that everyone else had: Rhys Roman was the richest man in Saint Sabine, and some argued, the richest man in all of New England. No one seemed able to nail down his exact age, though the media suspected he was early thirties. While the Roman family name had always been a prominent one in the city, Rhys came on the scene out of nowhere about eleven years ago.

He quickly proved to be a powerful figure and bought a bunch of crumbling buildings on the northern side of the city, razed them, and built new commercial and residential spaces. From there, he invested in a few up-and-coming tech companies that were now worth millions, and then moved on to the arts scene and donated ten million to the Museum of Saint Sabine so it could expand and improve.

He was single as far as Emery could tell and had been for the last eleven years.

Not that that mattered.

Not at all.

"I'm gonna go grab a drink." Tanner had to shout to be heard over the music. "I'll ask the bartender if he knows anything."

"Okay. I think I'm going to use the restroom. I'll meet you back here in a minute."

They parted ways, and Emery skirted the perimeter of the club until she found a hallway with a sign hanging over its entrance. VIP ROOMS, the first sign said, and the second, RESTROOMS.

Here the swirling lights of the club couldn't quite penetrate, but low-lit sconces hung from the walls every ten feet or so. The pool of light they cast wasn't quite enough for her to see by, so she kept her hand on the wall as she stumbled into the darkness.

Up ahead, she could hear a door open and shut. Someone thought, *Need another drink,* then, *That was the best fuck I've had in a long time.*

Gross.

She sidestepped to make room for them to pass, and as she did, she crashed into a very tall, very solid figure.

Bouncing back with an umph, she teetered on her stilettos, and just when she thought she might topple over, a cold hand snatched her by the wrist and yanked her upright.

"I'm sorry," she said. "I didn't see you there."

"Likely on account of your weak, mortal eyesight."

"Excuse me?" She wrinkled her nose and looked up, and then up some more.

The guy must have been several inches over six feet. At first glance, his face was hidden in shadow, but then he shifted into a slant of light and Emery inhaled a sharp breath.

Goddamn.

Emery was immediately struck by the cut of the guy's cheekbones. Predatory was the only word she could come up with, and the word went right along with the vibrant blue eyes.

And when he turned that gaze on her, she was suddenly a little dizzy, a little delirious.

He licked his lips, the wetness glinting in a rogue ray of light.

"I don't have weak eyesight," she threw back at him, trying to get her bearings. "I have 20/20 vision. It's just dark in here."

"Mmm," he said, as if he was suddenly bored.

Just who did this guy think he was anyway? He probably ate cereal in his underwear and laughed at his own burps, though truth be told, he'd look damn fine doing it.

Whenever Emery was feeling particularly lowly next to a hot-as-sin man, she focused on his thoughts to feel better. No guy was perfect. Not even this one. He must have some embarrassing secrets he was hiding.

Except...when she turned her focus on him, all she found was silence.

She squinted, brow furrowed.

What the heck was going on?

"Is something the matter?" the guy asked.

Oh shit, he was British too?

And there was something old about the deep rumble of his voice, the smooth, formal way he spoke. Something that Emery apparently liked because, despite the heavy heat of the club, a shiver raced down her body, nipples peaking, heat spreading between her thighs.

What the hell was happening? She wasn't the type to fawn over a hot guy, even if his face was godlike and his voice like sin.

And why the hell couldn't she hear his thoughts?

She barely had to try on most days.

"Little lamb," he said, his voice turning almost into a purr, "perhaps it's time for you to go."

"Huh?"

He hunched closer, his forearm propped on the stone wall. His breath smelled like whisky and rye.

Emery could have sworn his eyes glowed brighter, like a sapphire put in the sun.

But that must have been the club lights, a trick of the eye.

"I said, *you should go*." His voice rumbled with danger.

The hair at the back of Emery's neck stood on end. She suddenly felt like a child who had stumbled into the wrong dark forest.

Come closer, little one, and let me eat you up.

Emery took a step back. The guy mirrored her, moving with a speed and gracefulness that was eerily unnatural.

Everything about him was contradictory. He was telling her to leave with his words, but his body was saying something else, edging closer, his energy almost drawing her in.

The guy says to leave, you should probably leave.

But she was suddenly trapped in the ocean-glow of his eyes and the ripple of heat sinking below her belly.

When she exhaled, it came out sounding more like a sigh.

The guy came closer still. A breath stuttered down Emery's throat.

"Emery!" Tanner called from the end of the hallway.

She blinked and pulled back.

Even over the thud of her heart and the rapid drum of music, she could hear Tanner's thoughts as if spoken aloud.

Getting weird vibes from that guy, Tanner was thinking. *Emery might be in trouble.*

As much as she hated her boss, he always stood up for her in these kinds of situations.

One time, an ad exec slapped her on the ass after a meeting, and Tanner made the guy apologize, then put him on unpaid leave for two weeks.

She was always grateful for this kind of decency, especially from her boss, but she hadn't needed it...had she?

Emery looked up at the guy and found him staring at Tanner with an expression sharp enough to pierce flesh.

"Emery, there you are," Tanner said as he trotted up, drink in hand. "I was—" He glanced up at the mystery guy and cut himself off.

His mouth dropped open as his eyes got wide.

"Rhys," Tanner said. "Rhys Roman?"

Holy shit!

That was Rhys Roman?!

"Have we met?" Rhys said, his voice deep and gravelly, not bothering to hide his annoyance.

"Not yet." Tanner held out his hand. "I'm Tanner Jenison of—"

"TS Jenison," Rhys answered quickly.

"You know me!"

Tanner just went from protecting my honor to throwing a

celebratory party in Rhys's *honor.*

As Tanner babbled on about how much he admired Rhys and Roman Enterprises, Rhys turned his attention back to Emery. Except this time, his gaze was scrutinizing, as if he was searching her face for something specific.

Emery fidgeted beneath the weight of his attention and tucked a stray lock of hair behind her ear, and as she did, Rhys's eyes sunk to her throat.

Heart pounding like a wild thing in her chest, Emery swallowed hard and tried to catch her breath.

Rhys's nostrils flared. His pupils somehow dilated despite the darkness in the hallway.

Emery's head went a little swimmy again.

If she didn't know any better, she'd think she was drunk. But she hadn't had a drink yet. Had she? Everything about this night was turning into a smudge.

"You have time for a chat?" Tanner asked.

Rhys blinked away, and Emery jolted awake as if she were a snake, hypnotized beneath Rhys's intense gaze.

Seriously, what the hell was wrong with her?

"Come," Rhys said and disappeared into the shadows, his voice slithering out. "I have a VIP room this way."

Tanner widened his eyes at Emery, the excitement as clear on his face as it was in his head.

Fuck yeah. We're doing this!

Rhys led them down the hallway to an empty VIP room done up in rich plum and black velvet.

When the door shut behind them, tension flared up between Emery's shoulder blades, flight instinct roaring in her veins.

Did everyone feel this way around Rhys? If so, it was no wonder his reputation was so grand. The guy was intimidating as hell.

"Sit," Rhys said as he went to the mini bar in the back corner.

Tanner dutifully sat, his thoughts bouncing all over the place.

Roman's got great hair. Damn. How does he get it to look casual and shit, but polished at the same time? I've tried all the pomades. Nothing works like that on my hair. Wonder where he bought that shirt. Dude wears a plain black Tee and somehow looks like a king.

Emery admired the way the t-shirt in question skimmed the rise and valleys of Rhys's biceps, how it hung off his torso, hinting at a flat plane of ab muscles. She could only imagine what he looked like with that shirt off.

Everything about Rhys Roman was sexy and so fucking masculine.

"What do you drink?" Rhys asked over a shoulder as he slung back a shot of something dark.

"Oh uh...whatever you're having," Tanner said.

"I assure you, Mr. Jenison, you don't want what I'm having."

Tanner laughed. "Okay, bourbon on the rocks."

I might be out of my league, Tanner thought. *No, fuck that. I'm getting this deal. You can do this. Hammerhead shark! You've got this.*

Sometimes Tanner's internal pep talks were enough to make Emery want to vomit. And sometimes, like now, she felt a little sorry for him. He had no idea Emery was spying on his private thoughts.

If someone got inside her head, she'd die of mortification. She spent a ridiculous amount of time daydreaming about Twizzlers and fuzzy pajamas and knee-high cozy socks. And sometimes, when she was really bored, she got caught up in a fantasy of hooking up with the anti-hero from her favorite TV show. The scenarios were always different, but the imaginary sex was top notch.

"And you, Miss...." Rhys trailed off and looked at Emery over his shoulder. The golden light from one of the wall sconces hit his face just right highlighting the strong jaw, that sinful mouth.

"Just Emery," she said. "And I'll have whisky neat if you've got it."

He didn't answer, so she took that as confirmation that he did.

"Is this your VIP room?" she asked as he poured the drinks. She needed to focus on the business at hand, and it might be useful to know later on if Emery ever needed to hunt him down again.

"Club Shade is mine," he said, his back still to them. "So yes."

Did Tanner know that? Tanner lifted a shoulder at her and shook his head. Apparently not. The club wasn't in Rhys's public real estate portfolio.

Two glasses in hand, he came over and offered them the drinks. As Emery took hers, her fingers brushed up against his, and a thrill ran through her.

If that's how her body reacted to just a brush of fingertips, she could only imagine what he might be able to do to her if his hand was elsewhere.

Just the suggestion had Emery rubbing her thighs together.

Rhys sat on the sofa across from them and spread his long arms over the back.

Even in repose, his biceps bulged against the sleeves of his shirt. Emery couldn't help but trace the run of veins winding over his hands, around his forearms. She'd always been a hands girl. The veinier the better.

"Mr. Jenison," Rhys said, "what is it you wanted to talk about?"

Tanner leaned back on the sofa to match Rhys's casualness. This was one of his tactics, to mirror a potential business partner to instinctively tell the other they were on the same level.

Emery seriously doubted it'd work on someone like Rhys.

No one was on his level.

"First," Tanner said, "let me say that I, and my board, have been impressed with what you've done with Roman Enterprises. The expansion you did in Culver Park was exactly what that area needed, and the architectural choices you made were spot on. We want to work with someone of your caliber, and I hope you don't mind me being so forward about it. We'd love to pitch you some of our ideas if you'd be open to hearing them."

"I'm not," Rhys said evenly.

Emery choked on her drink.

Inside his head, Tanner was repeating the same word over and over again.

Fuck. Fuck. Fuck.

"Can I ask why?" he tried.

Rhys sat up straight. His shoulders leveled out. His body went eerily still. There was something in the way he looked at them now that was distinctly superior. Like they were two ducks that had waltzed into his party, and now, he was growing bored with their quacking.

"You want to know why?" he said. "Because I know precisely what you want. I know what you all want. You want the vacant land on the southeast end of the city. I'll tell you what I've told everyone that's come before you. You can't have it.

"Do you think you have something unique to offer me? Do you think that you're somehow special? You're not. I've had this conversation with three dozen men who've come before you, and all of those men failed just as you will."

Rhys stood up. He towered over them.

Emery looked away as blood rose to her cheeks. The sheer size and power of him overwhelmed her.

He returned to the mini bar, and the lid on a decanter came out with a pop when Rhys pulled it out. He poured himself another shot of that dark, thick liquid and drank it.

With his back to them, Tanner looked over at Emery and bugged out his eyes like, *Do something! Help me!*

She cringed at him apologetically. Tanner brought her here to work her magic, but this cursed ability didn't seem to work on Rhys, and she didn't know what the hell to do about it.

And if she couldn't help Tanner, then her downfall would be epic. She'd be stuck in that dingy apartment with her cousin for the rest of her life.

The thought made her heart sink and her stomach ache.

Tanner scrubbed at his face, frustration in the hard set of his jaw.

Emery couldn't live the rest of her life in that shitty apartment.

She surged to her feet, crossed the room, and stopped just a few inches away from Rhys.

A chill came over her.

Being this close to him was doing funny things to her body. Her best friend Morgan had this theory that some men were just more attractive because they had far more beneath the surface than regular men.

"Like an iceberg," was how Morgan explained it.

Strength. Intellect. Magnetism. Raw power.

Rhys had all of those things and more.

He was the type of guy who could corrupt any woman given the chance. If he asked Emery to sink to her knees, would she do it? Thinking about his cock in her mouth made her suddenly wet. Not because she loved giving blowjobs but because of the way he was looking at her now like he was imagining the same thing.

"Emery," he said.

Her name came out of his mouth sounding like a command.

"Yes?" she answered.

"He desires my land," he said, and nodded his head at Tanner. The rest of him remained unmoved. "What do *you* want?"

"I...well...."

Her cheeks went hot. She swore his eyes flashed again.

"I want the same thing as Tanner."

But as soon as the words were out of her mouth, she wasn't exactly sure how true they were.

Yeah, she wanted the promotion, a higher salary, a better apartment, but...what it really came down to was she wanted something *more*.

If she was going to be alone for the rest of her life, she at least wanted to be alone in a life she liked.

And if she were being honest, she fucking hated everything about her life right now. This life chaffed, made her feel raw, made the world seem colorless.

She'd thought she was building something with Michael, only to realize just how easily it could all fall apart.

But the only way to make a better life, even if it was alone, was to nab this deal.

With or without her mind reading abilities, she needed to find a way through this.

It was time for a new tactic.

"Why have you held on to that land for so long?" she asked. "Is it for conservation reasons? Because if so, I can assure you our development team always—"

"It's not."

Okay, strike one.

She narrowed her eyes as if that somehow controlled her strange ability.

Work dammit!

She'd never had to think about reading someone's mind.

If getting inside their heads was a doorway, she never had to turn the knob. The door opened automatically to her.

"Is there anything that would change your mind?" she asked.

Rhys took a step closer bringing with him the smell of spice and musk.

Emery licked her lips. Rhys watched her do it, and everything inside of her coiled up tight like a spring, ready to pop.

"I don't think you know what you're getting into," Rhys said.

With anyone else, his words would have been an insult, but instead they came out sounding like a challenge, one that Emery wanted to rise to meet.

"I've been in this business for years. I assure you, Mr. Roman, I know what I'm doing."

Face still unreadable, he said, "No, you don't."

Frustration bubbled up inside of her. "Mr. Roman, I've helped oversee multi-million-dollar deals at TS Jenison. Mr. Jenison can attest that I'm integral to the team and—"

"Very well," Rhys said, cutting her off. "Show me what you do."

"Huh?"

How did anyone keep up with this man?

"Give me a tour of TS Jenison's offices." He took another step, closing the gap between them. There was nowhere for her to go. She was practically pressed against the wall as it was. "Show me what you do," he added in a low, sinister voice.

Now the challenge felt more like a trap.

And despite her better judgment, Emery was tingling all over and hot as hell. Being near Rhys was like toeing the edge of a suspension bridge, the wind rushing up, stealing her breath away.

Why the hell did Rhys Roman want to see some boring office building?

Tanner clapped behind her. "We can do that. We can definitely do that. Done."

Rhys turned away, and the absence of his gaze released Emery again, almost like a tether.

Tanner rubbed his hands together. "I would love to show you around TS Jenison."

"Not you," Rhys said.

Tanner frowned. "Excuse me?"

"I'd like Emery to be my guide."

Tanner looked at her like she was last week's bologna. "You want my *assistant* to show you around?"

"Yes."

"Why?"

"Because I don't like you."

Tanner puffed out a breath, completely caught off guard while inside he threw a mega tantrum. *Fucking fuck! This fucking guy! What the fuck kind of game is he playing? Who would have thought the infamous Rhys Roman would want to bang my secretary? Bet he's got some kinky dom fantasies or some shit.*

Emery choked on her spit, and it turned into a run of coughing.

Rhys turned back to her, a frown etched between his brows. "Are you all right?"

"What? Oh. Sure. Yeah. Totally fine."

His frown deepened.

Rhys did not want to have sex with her.

Though if he did....

No. Nope. Not letting her mind wander on that one. Rhys Roman was practically movie star hot. Greek God hot. So good looking, it almost hurt to look at him.

There was no way in hell he was interested in her.

"Do we have a deal, Mr. Jenison?" Rhys asked.

Tanner blew out a breath. "Okay. Sure." He came over, hand out to shake on the deal. "Emery can show you around TS Jenison—"

"Tomorrow," Rhys said.

"Sure, tomorrow," Tanner replied.

Apparently, whatever she had going tomorrow didn't matter.

The men shook. Emery zeroed in on Rhys's head again, trying to weasel her way in. She still came up against absolute silence.

With the deal struck, Rhys went to the door and pulled it open. The thumping music crashed in all at once. Several people ambled by in the hallway and peered in, until they saw who stood in the doorway. Then they righted their gaze and hurried away.

"Now if you'll excuse me," Rhys said.

"Of course." Tanner scurried around the coffee table as if he meant to walk out with Rhys, but by the time he reached the doorway, Rhys was already gone.

CHAPTER 4

RHYS

As soon as Rhys was out of the VIP room, he sucked in a breath like a drowning man.

That woman...

Who the fuck was she?

He'd nearly bit her right there in the hallway.

Sunk his hand to her ass, and his teeth into her throat...

He was rock hard.

And the bloodlust was making his vision go white around the edges, and his teeth ache in his gums.

Fucking hell.

And he wanted to see her again tomorrow?

She'd be lucky to last another hour with him.

What the fuck was he thinking?

But if she was *the* girl...

Rhys didn't believe in coincidences.

The Oracle told him he needed TS Jenison and the girl, and then he ran into Tanner Jenison with a girl.

Fuck fuck.

Rhys followed the darkened hallway to the rear exit. When he was finally standing in the alley a second later, surrounded by boxes and crates and rotting food, he felt significantly better. There was nothing but rats out here, and he wasn't that far gone—*yet*.

It took him less than two minutes to cross Second District on foot. He came up on House Roman through the garden.

Dane and Cole were in the back parlor with Kat sitting next to them, her hands hovering over Cole's chest.

"Well?" Rhys said.

Kat looked at him over her bare shoulder, vicious red lips turned down in a frown. She was a four-hundred-year-old witch bound to Rhys's house, and the only witch he trusted.

She was dressed in an off-the-shoulder black dress and heels that could pierce a heart. It was hard to tell what her plans might have been for the night. Kat was the type of woman who was always dressed to kill.

"He's okay for now," she said. "But I'm sensing a fracturing, like the curse is effecting him more."

Rhys turned away before any of them could see a hint of worry on his face.

Fucking hell.

Gums aching, Rhys went around the bar to the mini fridge tucked in the corner. He was fucking starving, and his head was pounding, and shit was going sideways. He needed to take the edge off.

Inside the fridge, he found chilled lemons and limes, along with several bottles of seltzer and two dozen blood bags. He pulled one out, popped off the top, and drank it back. His incisors lengthened as soon as the coppery taste of blood was washing over his tongue.

An image of Emery flashed in his mind.

A growl came out of him, unbidden.

He was about two seconds from running out the back door and back to that woman so he could tear her clothes off and—

Fuck.

It was getting worse. *He* was getting worse.

When the bag was empty, he tossed it in the trash and looked up. He found Kat and Dane and Cole staring at him.

"How are you?" Kat asked.

"I'm fine," Rhys growled.

"You keep saying that," Dane pointed out.

"And I'll keep saying it," he said. Because admitting to his weakness was never an option.

With his thumb, he wiped a drop of blood from the corner of his mouth and sucked it off. He already wanted more. He was hard and ravenous, and he wanted to fuck and eat and—

"Dane told me about the Oracle," Kat said when she came over to the bar. She grabbed the bottle of Johnny Black that had been sitting out then reached over the counter for a shot glass and poured one, handing it to him. "Drink," she ordered and leveled her gaze at him.

He frowned at her but took the shot back.

"You know what used to be in TS Jenison," she said and poured him a second.

Rhys downed that one too and then came out from behind the bar. He dropped into one of the leather side chairs, head hung back. "Of course I do."

"So what do you plan to do about it?" she asked.

"We'll break in after hours," Dane suggested, "and have a look around."

Cole, still a little drunk on the night's debauchery, said, "I like that idea."

"No one is breaking in." Rhys scrubbed at his eyes.

"Okay, so..." Dane trailed off, waiting.

"I already have an appointment at TS Jenison tomorrow."

Dane said, "That was fast. How'd you manage that?"

"I ran into Tanner Jenison when I was leaving Club Shade."

Rhys sensed the collective shift of energy in the room. It was shock, mostly, and misgiving.

"And the girl," Rhys added.

"Like *The Girl*?" Dane asked.

"If she wasn't The Girl, it would be an awfully big coincidence. She was with Tanner and she...."

Rhys trailed off as he tried to find the right word, the right description to adequately sum up Emery. She was in her twenties, short compared to him, just a few inches over five feet if he had to guess. She smelled like candy and heritage roses. She smelled sweet, but her clothing was in direct contrast to that, darker, sharper. Scent told more truth than clothing did, and it made Rhys wonder if she was both dark and sweet, or one trying to be the other.

He could show her dark things.

"She was what?" Kat asked. "You're leaving us all in suspense here."

Rhys slouched in the chair and folded his hands over his middle. "I don't know. I could have sworn I smelled some Ravenwood witch on her, but it was faint and didn't seem like it belonged to her. Perhaps there's a Ravenwood or two working at TS Jenison. Perhaps the girl will lead me to them."

Dane got up and grabbed his laptop from the nearby table. "What was her name?"

Rhys heard the whir of the computer's fan start up as Dane typed in his password.

"Emery."

Less than five minutes later, Dane had her full name and her online profile pulled up. "She likes *Under the Tuscan Sun*," he said, reading from her profile. "And *The Witcher*."

"I'll bet she does," Kat said with a grin.

"What's her surname?" Rhys asked.

"Emery Blake."

Kat crossed her arms over her chest. "Blake isn't an original Sabine family name. She married?"

"Nope. Single."

Rhys's stomach churned.

"Does it say what her hometown is?" Kat asked.

"Saint Sabine, apparently."

Kat started to pace.

"What do you think?" Rhys asked.

"I suppose our theory that the girl could lead us to a Ravenwood is the most plausible. But that seems like an extremely thin connection for an Oracle to hand down. One might argue that if the girl is simply leading us to a Ravenwood, then she's not exactly the key to unlocking the curse, now is she? She'd just be the path."

Kat continued to pace as she thought. "Let's go over that night again," she said. "The night the curse was wrought. Tell me the exact—"

A chill crept into Rhys's shoulders. He hated rehashing that night.

He pushed off the chair and rose to his feet. "I have to go."

"What, now?" Kat said. "But the girl—"

"Trace her family lineage. Start there." He went for the door.

"Where are you going?" Dane asked.

"To rip out the throat of some drunken asshole," he said, resigned to it. If he was going to lose his fucking mind and give in to the bloodlust, he might as well do the world a favor while he was at it.

"Don't stay out too late, Dad," Cole yelled with a laugh.

"Fuck off," he said and then disappeared into the night.

CHAPTER 5

EMERY

After Club Shade and the whole encounter with Rhys Roman, all Emery wanted to do when she got home was put on her black leggings and her threadbare Yellowstone sweatshirt she'd inherited from her mother and curl up on the couch for some feel-good TV while she got drunk on wine and cracked open her five-pound tub of Twizzlers.

Unfortunately for her, when she walked in the door, she found her cousin and aunt at the rickety dining room table in some kind of heated discussion about something Emery was sure she didn't care about.

Her aunt and cousin stopped talking and looked up at her.

Beth had a beer in hand, condensation dripping down the amber glass. The apartment had no air conditioning, which was why Emery spent most of her time in her bedroom in front of her high-capacity fan.

"Hey," Emery said as she hung her keys on the hook by the door.

"Hi," Beth answered.

"Hello, darling," Aunt Nina said.

Nina and Beth were relatives on Emery's dad's side and while she'd never met the man (he took off before Emery was even born—because of that, no one even spoke his name), Nina and Beth had always been involved in Emery and her mother's lives.

But while Emery grew up with Beth, they'd never exactly been friends.

Emery got the impression that Beth looked at her like she was somehow beneath her, which annoyed Emery to no end considering it was Emery that had always excelled in school, and it was Emery that had been consistently employed since she was sixteen. By contrast, Beth barely graduated, and she couldn't hold down a job if her life depended on it.

The only reason she had an apartment was because her mother owned the building and let Beth live there for free.

It irked Emery that Beth barely had to put in the effort and somehow still had more than Emery did right now.

"What are you guys up to tonight?" Emery asked.

Aunt Nina came to Emery's side, brushing a stray lock of hair behind Emery's ear. "Just wanted to check in on my two favorite girls. How are you, dear?"

Aunt Nina was a lot kinder to Emery than Beth was, but Emery still got the impression that Nina didn't exactly *love* Emery. She tolerated her.

Maybe it was some kind of family duty Aunt Nina thought she owed Emery, since it was her brother that took off one night and never came back.

"I'm fine," Emery said, but her mind instantly went to Rhys.

She was more than fine. She was practically soaring, and she wanted some wine to celebrate.

Seems tired, Nina's thoughts said. *Looks pale.*

Emery frowned at her aunt's thoughts. She did not look pale!

Well...she was careful not to spend too much time in the sun. It wasn't like she needed skin cancer on top of being homeless.

She stepped around her aunt and opened the fridge. The light flickered, strobing over the boxes of takeout food, old condiments, and moldy cheese.

Emery's bottle of red blend was nowhere in sight. "Do you know where my wine is?"

Beth's eyes were on her phone as she scrolled through a feed. "Haven't seen it," she said while her thoughts said, *I drank it. Wine was a lot better than this beer.*

Rage burbled in Emery's chest.

Fucking hell.

The odd thing about Beth's internal chatter was how little she actually thought about Emery when Emery was consumed by her never-ending annoyance aimed at her cousin.

Did Beth really think so little of Emery that she barely thought of her at all?

Emery turned back to the fridge as if double checking, as if she didn't know exactly where the wine had been when she left before her meeting.

Should she say something?

Aunt Nina might take her side. Sometimes she could surprise Emery.

But no, in the end, it wasn't worth it, and Emery *was* tired.

With a sigh, Emery grabbed a bottle of water from the fridge. "Just as well. I don't need a hangover for tomorrow."

Not when so much was at stake. Not when she was about to spend alone time with Rhys Roman.

Her stomach lit with butterflies.

"Big day tomorrow?" Aunt Nina asked, sharp brow raised in question.

"Every day is a big day, Aunt Nina." Emery headed for her bedroom.

Every day was another chance for Emery to turn things around so she could escape this hell she found herself in.

"You take care of yourself, darling," Aunt Nina said.

Hah. Like Beth took care of herself?

"I will. Thanks Aunt Nina."

Emery made a quick exit and went into her bedroom, shutting the door behind her.

She had better things to turn her mind to.

Like Rhys Roman.

He had consumed her thoughts since leaving Club Shade. The entire ride back to the office with Tanner, she'd barely heard Tanner's internal ranting because all she could see and hear and think about was Rhys Roman.

What was it about that guy that was so... Emery tried to come up with a word that summed it up, and all she could think of was *devouring*.

The way his gaze raked over her like he wanted to possess her. The way his eyes seemed to light up, like he was excited by just the sight of her.

It made Emery feel a little delirious, like she'd do just about anything he asked of her.

Setting her phone on her dresser, she popped in her wireless earbuds and called her best friend Morgan.

Morgan picked up on the second ring. "Hi," she said, her face turned away from the camera.

"I had a wild night and I need to tell someone about it."

"Go on." Morgan's dark, curly hair was wild around her face. There was a slight pink to her cheeks which told Emery her best friend was at least halfway through a bottle of wine. Morgan always got a little flushed with wine.

Morgan was still turned away from the camera, her eyes shifting over whatever lay before her.

"What are you doing right now?" Emery asked.

"A puzzle." Morgan held up the front of the box. It was a spread of vintage cameras. For Morgan, the picture didn't matter so much as the challenge. She loved a good puzzle. In another life, Morgan could have easily been Lara Croft or a Goonie.

"Well, put your puzzle aside," Emery said. "Because you're going to want to hear this."

"I assure you, I can do a puzzle and listen at the same time, but go ahead." She set her chin in the cup of her hand and turned her attention to Emery. "This better be good."

"I met Rhys Roman tonight."

Morgan straightened. Her eyes got a little wider. "Oh?"

"He was every bit as intriguing as you thought he'd be."

Morgan wasn't into the superstitions or the mysticism that her mother or grandmother had been when she was growing up, but she did love a challenge. She'd always been intrigued by Rhy's ability to stay off social media and there-fore, stay unknown.

"He's British, did you know that?" Emery said.

"Really? That's weird, right? Since the Roman family has been in Saint Sabine pretty much since it's incorporation."

"It definitely caught me off guard."

"Okay, so what did he say? What did he do?"

Emery broke down the encounter, starting with the intense meeting in the hallway before Tanner showed up.

"And then he asked me to show him around the office tomorrow," Emery finished. "Me. Not Tanner. Can you believe that?"

"Yes," Morgan said. "But I bet Tanner was blowing a gasket."

Oh she had no idea.

While Emery suspected that if she told Morgan she could read minds, she'd believe her, she didn't want her friend to avoid her. Morgan was an extremely private person, extraordinarily hard to get close to. She didn't trust easily, and she guarded her heart as if it were the Crown Jewels.

Emery didn't want to rock the boat, so to speak.

Thankfully, Emery's ability had never worked over the phone, so right now, Morgan's thoughts were blissfully silent. And even when they were together, Morgan never had a cross thing to think about her.

"What are you going to wear tomorrow?" Morgan asked.

"I have no idea. Care to help a girl out?"

"Of course." Morgan grabbed her phone and walked with it across her apartment. She plopped down on her couch. String lights that hung from the ceiling glowed above her. "What was Rhys wearing tonight?"

"Plain t-shirt. Looked expensive though."

"Okay, so I'm guessing he likes understated luxury, so don't go bold. He's supposedly a billionaire, right? Billionaires can have whatever they want, including people, so don't try too hard."

Emery went to her tiny closet and flipped through hangers and pulled out a pair of skinny black chinos. She held them up in front of the phone. "What about these?"

"That might work." Morgan took a sip of her wine. "Oh, try those with that blood red silk blouse."

Emery undressed and pulled on the chinos, then grabbed the blouse from the closet and slid it on over her head. It was short-sleeved and the lightest fabric, so it felt like a soft caress against her skin.

It made her immediately think of Rhys bending closer in the darkness of the club hallway, and her nipples peaked.

Dammit. If this was how she reacted to just the thought of him, how the hell would she get through tomorrow?

She tried shaking him from her mind as she tucked the blouse into the pants and slid on a camel brown leather belt.

"Gorgeous," Morgan said, the glass of wine held close to her face. The flush was growing across her cheeks. "Hair in a ponytail. Wear some dangly earrings."

Emery opened her top dresser drawer where she stashed her jewelry beneath several layers of panties. Beth never wore jewelry, but Emery wouldn't put theft past her if she simply wanted to piss Emery off.

The jewelry was stored in a compartment box, so she popped the top and scanned the options. She went with a pair of gold thread earrings.

"So Rhys Roman," Morgan said, "was he a smug bastard? If I were a hot billionaire, I'd be a smug bastard. Wait, was he hot?"

Emery turned to check her reflection in the cheap dollar store mirror she'd hung on the back of her bedroom door. "Ridiculously hot. And smug bastard..." She thought of the way he bluntly told Tanner he didn't like him. "Smug isn't the right word. Maybe..." Emery chewed on her bottom lip as she thought. "Ruthless comes to mind."

"Mmmm." Morgan downed the rest of her wine and set

the glass aside. "I wonder what fucking a hot ruthless billionaire is like. You think he takes all of the attention?"

Emery flashed to the hallway again, to Rhys's closeness, to the way he dominated her and her space. The obvious answer seemed like yeah, he'd take all of the attention, but there was a nagging feeling in the back of her mind that he might like making her beg for it instead.

And thinking that made her clit throb.

Emery swallowed and turned away from the phone. "Hard to say. I suppose I should get to bed early and make sure I get some rest for tomorrow."

Morgan shook the empty wine glass in front of the phone. "And I'm empty and I have a puzzle to finish."

Emery laughed. "What a wild life you lead."

"Wild and intense. Fill me in tomorrow afterward, okay?"

"You know I will."

They said goodbye, and Emery ended the call. She rehung the outfit and left the earrings on her dresser so everything was ready for the morning.

And as she lay in bed, the TV in the living room droning on and on, she slowly drifted off to sleep, hoping and praying that tomorrow went well and that Rhys Roman would finally give in—to Emery of all people—and strike a deal with TS Jenison. And maybe finally, *finally*, Emery could escape this apartment once and for all.

CHAPTER 6

EMERY

Emery had made sure to set her alarm early so she had plenty of time to get ready. She came out of her room just a little after eight, and as she tip-toed down the hallway, she paused at her cousin's open bedroom door.

That was odd. Beth was never up before noon. In fact, Emery was convinced her cousin didn't even realize eight a.m. existed.

She popped her head through the open door just to make sure Beth wasn't on the floor, drowning in a pool of her own vomit, but nope, the room was empty, the bed unmade.

Where the hell did Beth go at eight in the morning?

Not my problem. And I don't care.

Emery headed out.

After stopping at the local café for a latte, she made it to the office fifteen minutes before nine. Tanner hadn't arrived yet, not surprisingly. He usually sauntered in closer to ten.

She busied herself filing some paperwork she hadn't

finished the day before, then made some copies of a contract that needed to be mailed out.

Every now and then, Emery would check the elevator across the office space, hoping to catch sight of one very tall, very hot billionaire.

The entire office was going to lose their minds when they saw him, and when they realized he was there for Emery...

She wasn't big on the whole popularity thing that inevitably went on in an office setting, but damn if she wouldn't bask in the glow of it!

At a little past eleven, Tanner finally showed up with bags beneath his eyes and a scowl on his face. He'd apparently gone out last night after they'd parted ways. He'd been in a horrible mood after their meeting with Rhys and had even whined, "Why the hell doesn't Rhys Roman want *me* to give him a tour?" as he sped uptown.

As if Rhys hadn't already answered that.

Truth was, Emery knew more about TS Jenison than Tanner did. He probably couldn't even locate the copy machine if someone pointed a gun at his head.

Tanner shut himself in his office and didn't reappear until one, and when he did come out and show his face, he said, "I'm leaving for the day. Don't fuck up the meeting with Rhys."

"It's just a tour," Emery said. "There isn't much to it."

Tanner looked at her. His thoughts pinged through his head. *Rhys is a fucking asshole. Hate that guy. Maybe I should stay to watch out for Em.*

For the briefest of seconds, Emery softened to Tanner's bad mood. But then he thought, *Nah. Rhys can have any woman he wants. No way he'd waste his time with Emery. I'm gonna go get drunk instead.*

"I'll see you tomorrow," Tanner said and left.

With her boss gone, Emery tried distracting herself with the internet. She did a new search on Rhys Roman, but she'd already read every article listed on the first seven pages of the results.

Her eyes kept straying from the screen to the elevator bank.

The clock tick-tocked in the background. People started leaving for the day, their computers shutting down, their desk lamps clicked off.

Was Rhys standing her up?

When the clock read nearly six, Emery's high hopes crashed and burned.

Served her right. Morgan was always telling her she was too naive, that she too often gave people the benefit of the doubt when what they really needed was a middle finger.

Of course Rhys Roman wasn't coming to see her, specifically.

Of course Rhys Roman had stood her up because—

Her office phone rang.

No name showed up on the caller ID.

Not unusual, but certainly interesting considering it was after hours.

She picked up the receiver and said a tentative, "Hello, Tanner Jenison's office, this is Emery."

"Emery," a deep, dark voice said on the other end.

The hair at the back of her neck stood up, and butterflies filled her belly. "Mr. Roman," she replied because she'd know that voice anywhere now. She could be blind in a tornado, and she'd still know that voice.

"I must apologize," he said. "I'm running behind today. Are you still at the office?"

"Oh yeah, totally. I'm always here late."

Half true. She didn't stay if she could get away with it. She didn't love her job *that* much. But more often than she'd like to admit, she was the one picking up the slack with the hopes that it'd someday pay off.

There was Morgan's voice again in the back of Emery's mind, reminding her that if she wasn't careful, she'd slowly transform into a doormat.

"What time were you thinking?" Emery asked.

"After sunset."

After sunset was a weird way to make an appointment.

"Sounds good. I'll be here."

"I'll see you then," he said and hung up.

EMERY WATCHED the sun set behind the city's skyline, and her heart kicked up. And when the light flicked on over the elevator to indicate the car was moving upward, Emery thought she might barf right there on her desk.

He didn't stand her up after all.

And he seriously wasn't lying about that whole *after sunset* thing.

With only a few minutes to spare, she hurried to the cabinet in her office and yanked open the door. There was a small locker mirror adhered to the back of the door, and Emery gave herself a quick once over. She looked all right for having spent the entire day waiting like a sucker for Rhys to show up.

Lips pulled back in a wide grin, she checked her teeth, then cupped her hand over her mouth and breathed into it. She didn't detect any of the onion she'd had on her salad from lunch, so that was good. She'd been kicking herself for that all day.

How good was Rhys's sense of smell? Maybe she should pop in a piece of gum just in case. But before she could locate the pack in her purse, the elevator dinged, and the doors slid open, and suddenly, Emery was staring at Rhys Roman across the wide expanse of cubicles.

The world narrowed.

Goosebumps erupted on Emery's arms. Her throat constricted.

When the day had dragged on, and she hadn't seen or heard from Rhys, she started to worry she'd imagined the whole exchange from the day before. She liked getting lost in ridiculous fantasies in her head. Whenever Emery got in trouble in school as a kid, it was always for not paying attention.

"She's a daydreamer, this one," her mother would explain to the principal. "She might grow up to be a writer someday. You should encourage daydreaming if you want my opinion."

The principal never did. Emery got more than one detention for drifting off in the middle of class, eyes wide open, but mind far gone. When you spent the majority of your day hearing everyone's thoughts, the only way to escape the hellhole was to disappear.

But she hadn't made this up, because Rhys was here.

And now...well, *he was here,* and she needed to do something about it.

She waved at him across the office and made her way through the cubicles while silently thinking *don't trip don't trip* over and over again to burn it into her subconscious.

Tanner would have a field day with that news. "You had one job," he'd say, "and you couldn't even cross the room without screwing it up!"

Thankfully, she made it without any mishaps. Mark that one down in the books as a success.

Now on to the next.

"Hey," she said when she and Rhys met in the middle of the office.

Music played through the building sound system, but it was quiet and faraway to Emery's ears as she took in the sight of Rhys.

Tonight, he wore black jeans, a black t-shirt, and a plain black bomber jacket. Blond stubble covered his face, and his dirty blond hair was raked over in a way that was very lux and very casual all at the same time.

He smelled like a dark summer night.

An hour ago, she might have been annoyed that she had to stay late, but now she couldn't imagine being anywhere else other than right here.

Emery was never one for puzzles, not like Morgan, but for some reason, she wanted to figure out the enigma that was Rhys Roman.

"Hey," she said. "You found me."

"So I have." His face was blank. He didn't seem as excited to see her as she was to see him. Then again, they were trying to talk him into parting with his land, and he'd already told them no, so...

Emery had to crane her neck to look up at him. In the artificial lighting of the office space, his bright blue eyes almost looked white.

"Well," Emery turned away and spread out her arm like she was a game show host, "this is where the magic happens. TS Jenison's admin offices. Architecture and design are on the fourth floor. Human resources and customer service are on the third floor and..."

She turned back to Rhys. He wasn't looking out to the office. Instead, his eyes were trained firmly on her.

Her stomach dropped to her heels.

Fuck.

When he looked at her, she wanted to light her panties on fire and swing them around her head.

Okay no. That was insane.

Get it together.

"Sorry, you wanted a tour, not a breakdown of our floor plan. Where would you like to start?"

"Let's start at the bottom and work our way up. I understand the building is one of the oldest in Saint Sabine, and I do love history."

Seeing an opportunity to seize onto something he actually was interested in, Emery said loudly, "Oh! Yes!" She pulled back and cleared her throat. "Yes, the original building is the basement and the next two floors. If it's history you want, the basement is a great place to start."

"After you." He stepped back to allow her into the elevator. She went in and hit the B button. With Rhys beside her, the elevator doors slid closed. Now she was sealed in a tiny six-by-six box with him. His scent overwhelmed her. God, she could get lost in that scent.

She found herself taking in a deep breath of him without even realizing it.

Rhys leaned against the back wall next to her, hands in his jacket pockets. She stole a look at him out of the corner of her eye. She liked how his hair swooped over his forehead like a cresting wave. She liked the way his Adam's apple stuck out from his neck, the way his lips were just slightly parted like his tongue might flick out and down her...

His nostrils flared, and his gaze jetted to hers. As soon as his eyes were on her, glowing again, Emery's insides tensed like she'd just entered a dark room and couldn't find the light switch.

He sucked in a breath. Emery shivered.

No wonder Rhys was infamous in Saint Sabine. She'd only spent a handful of minutes with him by this point, and already, she could barely think straight.

But everything rested on this meeting.

She needed to summon some of Morgan's indifference.

Morgan would never fawn over someone like Rhys Roman.

The elevator settled on the basement floor, and the doors dinged open.

Emery blinked several times and cleared her throat. She could do this. There was a reason Rhys had requested her specifically, and she'd prove he'd chosen right.

"Come on." She stepped out into the main hallway. There were file storage rooms to the right and supply storage to the left. Straight ahead, there was an old access tunnel that used to lead to the Saint Sabine Bank & Armory next door. The bank had since been razed, and the tunnel was bricked-up. But it was a cool story that Rhys might appreciate.

She led him down the hall. On this end of the basement, TS Jenison hadn't bothered to install new fluorescent lights, so the old glass sconces were all they had to light the way. The bulbs glowed soft golden in the underground space.

As they walked, Emery told Rhys the story of how TS Jenison had once been rumored to be a speakeasy and then the headquarters of a mafia family. She wasn't sure if she actually believed them. It was her cousin that told her the stories, and Beth had always been a bullshitter.

"Which family?" Rhys asked as they reached the hall's end.

"The Wood family," she answered with pride.

"Wood family," Rhys said. "Yes, that's correct."

"So you did know," she said teasingly. "You were just testing me?"

He ran his hand over the mismatched bricks on the bricked-up tunnel. "I've been down here before and I've never seen this tunnel."

"Wait...you have? When?"

"A long time ago."

"Then why..." She narrowed her eyes at him. "Is this some kind of joke?"

He finally turned back to her. "I assure you, there is nothing funny about this."

"But what *is* this, exactly?"

Rhys leaned in closer to the bricked tunnel's archway as if he was listening for something. "Do you know what's on the other side?"

"No. I heard it was caved in."

"Are there any other boarded or bricked-up rooms in the basement?"

Emery frowned. "I don't think so?" How did this factor into him making a decision on his land?

"Want to head up and see the next floor?" she suggested "If you think these old bricks are cool, the Berber carpet in human resources is gonna blow your mind."

He turned to her, the first hint of a smile appearing on his lips. "What is the origin of this Berber carpet you speak so highly of? Is it eastern European? Northern Atlantic perhaps?"

At first, she'd been annoyed to think he was playing

some kind of game with her, but now, *if* that was the case, it felt as though Rhys were inviting her to the table.

She just had to figure out exactly what the game was. Maybe then she could win.

"Oh please." She waved haughtily at him. "Eastern European Berber is so last year. Ours was machine woven in a factory in central Ohio."

He laughed. Actually laughed, and Emery's insides lit up. When he looked at her next, there was new amusement in his eyes and something that looked an awful lot like interest.

"Why don't you show me this Berber carpet," he said.

"Of course. My pleasure. Right this way, Mr. Roman. Gird your loins."

"They are firmly girded."

Who would have thought the key to breaking down billionaire mystery man Rhys Roman's well-constructed walls was witty banter about Berber carpeting?

Tanner was so going to owe her when this was done. She was getting this deal, dammit. If it was the last thing she did.

CHAPTER 7

RHYS

RHYS HAD YET TO SEE ANYTHING THAT RESEMBLED A KEY THAT might break a century-old curse, but the bricked-up tunnel was certainly circumspect.

Rhys and Dane had broken into and scoured the TS Jenison building in the early 1900s, looking for anything that might have been left behind by the Ravenwood witches. There had been no tunnel in the basement. But that didn't mean it hadn't been there.

Any of the witch families were capable of casting an illusion.

The Ravenwood witches were particularly talented in the magic of nature, and brick was certainly an element of nature. Hiding the tunnel would have been an easy illusion for a Ravenwood.

The question was, why would the tunnel show itself now? Even if all of the Ravenwood witches were dead, the magic would still remain.

As Emery explained some of TS Jenison's operations and upcoming projects, Rhys found himself scrutinizing her.

If she was the girl the Oracle had mentioned at Club Shade, then who was she? And what could she give Rhys to fix this fucking curse?

As the elevator made its way back up to the fifth floor, Emery leaned against the back wall and chatted away about the new development in Central Fifth District. She was gesturing with her hands, her voice rising, her heart rate kicking up with her excitement. She liked talking about development and infrastructure, but more so about conservation and heritage preservation.

And her excitement had her blood pumping fast through her veins.

Rhys zeroed in on the burgeoning vein in her neck.

What would she taste like? Sweet or tart or tangy or—

The elevator door chimed open, and the night janitor blinked in at them from the fifth floor.

"Hey, Harry!" Emery said as she stepped off.

"Evening, Emery," Harry said and doffed his baseball cap to her. "You're here late."

"On a mission tonight, Harry. This is Mr. Roman. I was just showing him the magic behind the curtain."

Harry offered his hand. "Pleasure to meet you."

Rhys tamped down his sudden hunger and kept his mouth firmly closed to avoid flashing the growing sharpness of his incisors. He shook, said nothing. The old man frowned.

He had to be in his sixties, judging by the stoop to his back and the gray flecking his dark hair. But his heartbeat was strong, and Rhys could hear it in the back of his head.

A repetitive dah-dum, dah-dum.

"I'll get out of your hair," Harry said. "I only have the trash left to take out, then I'm done for the night. It was nice to see you Ms. Blake. And you Mr. Roman. You both enjoy your night."

"You too," Emery said.

Harry took the elevator they'd arrived in, and soon, he was gone.

Now it was just Rhys and Emery.

Now it was Emery's heart Rhys could hear beating in his head.

Rhys licked his lips as his teeth throbbed and his gums ached.

Fuck, he needed to get out of here. The blood lust had snuck up on him this time, and the line between Emery's safety and her neck being torn out by his teeth was starting to blur.

The need for blood was pounding at the back of his throat, overwhelming him. Emery was speaking, but her voice was far away.

Just one bite.

One bite couldn't hurt.

And then, maybe he'd shove her against the wall, and he'd fuck her and bite her and fuck her some more and—

Something rang in the background.

"I should get that," Emery said. "It might be Tanner." She turned away. "He's probably wondering if I treated you well."

Rhys knew trouble was coming the moment Emery turned away from him. He saw it in the dimpling of muscle along her back, and the loose bending of her knees as her body prepared to jog away to catch the phone call.

Rhys's nostrils flared. His vision tunneled, and adrenaline flooded his veins.

He tried to stop her. But he didn't try hard enough. Truth was, he wasn't sure he wanted to.

When Emery jogged across the office, Rhys gave in and chased after her.

CHAPTER 8

EMERY

One second Emery was hurrying through the cubicles, and the next she was weightless and flying like she was on a rollercoaster, the world a blur around her. When the world stopped spinning, she was clear on the other side of the office, and Rhys was pressed against her, his hand wrapped around her throat, long, cold fingers digging into the flesh along her jawline, forcing her to crank her head back.

What the fuck was going on?

How did—

"Don't. *Move*."

Rhys's voice was hoarse and strangled at her ear. Her heart kicked up. Rhys growled low in his throat, and Emery felt the sound rumble through his chest, that's how close he was to her.

"What are you—"

"Emery," he said, turning her name into a warning.

What was happening? Was Tanner actually right for once? Should she have asked him to stay with her?

Oh God.

This was about the only time in her life when she wished her ability to read minds wasn't malfunctioning. Maybe it would have clued her into the psychopathic billionaire.

Rhys closed his eyes, and his entire body trembled. "Emery," he said quietly. "I'm going to let you go. But I need you to listen to me."

"Okay," she squeaked.

Her mother, when Emery was a child, had sat her down and told her the dangers that lurked in the world. Don't go anywhere alone after dark. Do not walk down darkened alleys. Don't get into someone's car without knowing who they are and where they're going. Don't take candy from a stranger.

But her mother had never taught her a lesson about dark, handsome billionaire's playing weird games of domination in the office.

Because that's what this was, wasn't it?

Why else would Rhys be holding her hostage in his grip while simultaneously acting like he was fighting against himself for doing it?

None of this made sense.

And clearly, she was a gullible idiot who thought she might actually get to change the mind of Rhys Roman.

"When I let you go," he said, "I need you to leave."

"The office?"

"Yes."

"But my phone—"

"Leave it."

She gave a quick nod of her head. His grip loosened. Some of his weight lifted off of Emery, but she could sense how he struggled with it, as if his head was telling him to do one thing and his body was telling him to do another. Just like at Club Shade when they'd first met in the hallway.

"When I let you go," he said again, "don't run. Do you understand?"

She made the mistake of meeting his gaze and gasped at what she saw. His eyes were glowing again. There was no denying it this time. This wasn't a trick of the light or flashing lights in a nightclub.

His eyes were *glowing*.

That bright vibrant blue ringed in darkest black.

And worse, fangs protruded from his mouth. Like actual fangs.

What the hell?

Emery recalled years back, while sitting around a bonfire with friends, one of the girls, an occult fanatic, had told a story of vampires in Saint Sabine.

"They aren't the pale beasts from the old movies," the girl had said. "They're handsome, alluring, charming, and clever. The vampires of Saint Sabine are the monsters you never see coming."

But that was just a stupid story meant to scare, right?

Vampires weren't real.

Not real huh? So how do you explain the fangs?

Rhys, inhaling deeply, removed his hand from Emery's throat and took a step back.

Emery stood frozen waiting for direction.

"Walk slowly," he said.

Hands trembling at her side, she took a tentative step. The distance between her and the elevators looked like ten football fields.

She kept walking, one foot in front of the other.

She didn't dare look back, but she sensed the space

between her and Rhys widening. So he wasn't following her. That was good.

Every step through the cubicle maze was excruciating.

Sweat beaded at her temple. She couldn't catch her breath over the rapid beating of her heart.

Despite her slow pace, it was like she was an hour into an elliptical workout.

If she survived tonight, she'd do everything right from here on out. She'd start taking her mother's warnings seriously. She'd eat all the vegetables she could get her hands on. She'd start recycling consistently and donating to food banks. And she'd definitely not take candy from strangers. Oh, and she'd totally never again agree to meet a sexy-as-hell-but-also-dangerous billionaire in the office after hours.

Please just let me survive this...whatever game this is.

She no longer wanted to win. She just wanted to survive.

When she reached the elevator, Emery slowly stretched out her hand for the button. As she waited for the car to come up to the fifth floor, she sang "Bad Romance" in her head to distract herself.

Finally, the elevator doors pinged open, and Emery stepped inside. She slowly turned to the floor panel and hit the button for the ground floor.

And just before the doors slid closed behind her, she looked out across the office and couldn't see Rhys anywhere. She pushed repeatedly at the DOORS CLOSED button. "Come on. Come on."

There was no movement from the office. No indication of where Rhys had gone.

When the doors slid closed, Emery deflated against the back of the car.

CHAPTER 9

RHYS

RHYS RAN.

He crossed seven miles from the north end of Saint Sabine to the south end, back to the Second in less than three minutes. He grabbed the first poor sap he could find and sunk his teeth into the man's neck just to quell the thundering hunger in his head and in his gut. The guy barely fought him.

The bloodlust pounding through his veins settled but did not relent. The man's blood was tangy and sharp as Rhys drank it back.

When the guy's heart slowed, Rhys disengaged and dropped the man in an alley behind a dumpster.

An image of Emery came back to him. The scent of her fear. The sound of her laughter. The staccato beat of her heart.

The hunger returned. Rhys's skin was on fire, but he was ice cold to the touch.

He needed more.

He needed more.

He sped from the alley and found another unfortunate soul.

When that vein was tapped, he grabbed a man in a heated argument with another and drank him too.

He couldn't stop.

The monster had a firm hold on him, and Rhys worried that no amount of blood would ever sate him again.

RHYS WOKE with the pointed end of a boot in his ribs.

He rolled over, dizzy, achy, and pissed. He was going to murder whoever dared to rouse him.

But when he opened his eyes, he saw Kat on the other end of the boot with Dane standing beside her.

"Have a fun night, did you?" Dane said.

Rhys scrubbed at his face and then stared up at the ceiling. He was in his bedroom. That was a good sign. He'd woken in more than one unfamiliar place in his lifetime.

What the fuck happened last night? His memories were murky and distant.

He propped himself up on his elbows and looked around. All he could smell was blood. He was covered in it. But from what he could tell, he was alone in the room, other than Kat and Dane. Another good sign.

Rhys swung his legs over the side of the bed and put his elbows to his knees. He scratched at his head and then realized his hands were bloodstained. He needed a fucking shower.

"What happened?" Kat asked.

"I was at TS Jenison with Emery and then—"

Fuck. Emery.

He jolted upright. The room swam and his head pounded. Too much blood. Too much liquor-soaked blood. But while he was regretting getting drunk on drunks, he was glad he'd had enough sense not to go on a murder spree.

In the twenty-first century, it was getting harder and harder to cover that shit up.

"I have to call Emery."

Why? Why the fuck did he care what he'd done?

He shouldn't care, and yet, he did.

He wanted to apologize to her. He wanted to explain himself, though the shape of that excuse was still unknown to him. He'd revealed some of his vampiric side. It would be hard to come back from that.

Kat put her hand out to stop him. "Slow down. The girl can wait." Kat didn't have the physical strength to restrain him, but she definitely had the magic.

Kat was a Redheart witch, and the Redhearts had a talent for magic of the body. Healing. Wounding. Exploding hearts, blowing brains. But her magic didn't work the same on a vampire, in particular one as old as Rhys.

Dane dropped into one of the wingback chairs by the open balcony doors. It was night still? Or maybe night again. That made much more sense. Which meant Emery had spent the entire day likely grappling with what had transpired the night before. Rhys was surprised the police weren't banging down his door.

Dane popped open the top on a bag of blood. The cold stuff was nowhere near as good as blood tapped from the vein, but it did in a pinch.

"If this Emery girl is the key to breaking the curse," he said, "I hope you didn't go and suck and fuck her. We don't need that kind of damage right now."

Rhys sped across the room, yanked the bag out of Dane's

grip and downed it. When he came back up for air, Dane was frowning at him.

"I have more, asshole," Dane said. "All you had to do was ask."

Next to Ramses, Dane was Rhys's oldest friend, and now that Rhys and his Turned were suffering from the Ravenwood curse, Rhys was lucky to have Dane by his side. The curse only effected Rhys's line. Right now, he needed someone clear headed. Especially since he hadn't seen Ramses in nearly two months.

Dane and Rhys met over four hundred years ago on a battlefield in northern Europe. It was Dane's sword that had been stabbed through Rhys's gut.

When they realized they were both vampires, Rhys broke Dane's neck and left him face down in the mud.

Their tit-for-tat killing and maiming of each other went on for another ten years before they called a truce and shared a round of drinks to toast to it.

They'd been best friends ever since.

Where Rhys was menacingly patient, stubborn and driven, Dane was an arrogant, egotistical tech genius who took what he wanted and never apologized. He was easily amused, relentless in his quests, and extremely loyal.

Despite the fact that he wasn't a Turned of House Roman, he'd always been loyal to Rhys, almost to a fault.

"If there are more blood bags," Rhys said, "then what the fuck are you complaining about?"

Dane sighed. "Chipper as always."

Kat curled her hand around her hipbone and arched a dark brow at him. "Tell me you didn't bite the poor girl from Jenison's?"

"I didn't bite her," Rhys growled.

But he sure as hell fucking wanted to.

It was a goddamn miracle he'd made it out of that office building without attacking her.

"Okay, so what *did* you accomplish?" Kat asked. "Did you find anything noteworthy in that building?"

Rhys tore off his bloody shirt and tossed it in the garbage. He'd have to incinerate half his bedroom from the looks of it. "There's a bricked tunnel in the basement that I think was glamoured the last time Dane and I examined the building. Could be something important on the other side."

"Okay. So what's your plan?" Kat asked.

They would go after hours and enthrall the security guard. And if they did that, Rhys could avoid seeing Emery.

But did he want to? Shouldn't he say something to her?

No. He should just let it go. Let her go.

Unless she was *the girl*. Unless she was the one mortal he needed to fix this damn curse.

But why her? He couldn't find or sense anything special about her.

"Did you find out anything on Emery?" he asked.

Dane grabbed a second bag of blood. "Still working on it. Her last known address was listed in Heath, but the apartment is leased to someone else now. And her surname dead ends at her grandmother."

"We're looking into it," Kat said. "You said she smelled like a Ravenwood witch. Did you get anything more on that?"

Rhys disappeared into his closet and pulled a fresh t-shirt from a hanger. "Oddly enough, no." He came back out to face them. "In fact, the scent was completely gone."

"Maybe another illusion?" Dane suggested.

It was certainly possible. Could she have been playing him this entire time?

Anger at the thought sharpened in his gut.

If she'd deceived him, he'd make her regret it.

"Have you ever wondered if Ciri is just sending you on a wild chase so the clock winds down in the background and you just wipe yourselves out?" Dane said. "The whole Roman House in one swoop?"

Rhys grumbled. "Of course I've considered it."

Ciri and her Oracles owed him nothing. But it was in everyone's best interest that Rhys's Turned vampires kept their sanity. It would be bloodshed and chaos if all of them went mad. Especially Rhys.

The Ravenwood family had never cared about the lives of mortals or vampires, and now the curse they cast long before the modern era was going to have even bigger ramifications, considering how the world now operated.

It would be disastrous.

If there was any shred of truth to the Oracle's prognostication, Rhys had to follow it.

Which meant he had to return to TS Jenison and knock down that wall.

But how the fuck did Emery factor into this?

The wall first, then he could deal with Emery.

"What time is it now?" he asked. His phone was nowhere in sight.

"Just a little after seven," Kat answered.

"Perfect. Then we should get started. You both are coming with."

Kat rolled her eyes. "I don't get my hands dirty. You know that."

He turned to her. The air crackled around her. She sensed him ready to spring. There was no such thing as subtlety where Kat was concerned. She could read Rhys like a map.

"You're coming with, Kat."

"I'm not one of your Turned. You don't get to boss me around."

He shot across the room.

Kat might have had all of the advantages in the world—she was immortal, magical, and familiar with Rhys and all his tricks—but she was no match for a vampire's speed.

He had her around the throat before she could react. She gritted her teeth. The air vibrated with her magic, and the hair along Rhys's arms lifted, electric.

"You're coming with," he bit out, his fangs grazing his bottom lip.

Kat snorted. "Or what?"

It was funny, the challenge in her voice. As if he didn't have a hundred and one things to use against her and only half of them violent.

He smirked down at her. "Or I'll tell your mortal descendants where to find your gold."

Horror washed across her face. "You motherfucker!" She laid her hand on his forearm and zapped him. The magic burned through his bones, singeing his skin leaving blackened flesh in its wake.

He dropped her and shook out his arm as the skin healed itself.

Kat clucked at him. Dane laughed.

"Now I have to move my gold," she said.

"As if I couldn't sniff it out again," he argued.

"It's my gold, goddammit."

"It's doing no one any good buried in the ground!"

She harrumphed and crossed her arms over her chest. "They'd just piss it away anyway. Have you seen what Brooke is driving these days? A Mustang! She has three kids under seven!"

"Children, children," Dane said. "We can argue about

gold and descendants some other time. Right now, let's focus on the task at hand, shall we?"

"Yes, let's," Rhys said. "Now that we're aligned in our mission," Kat grumbled, "I'm taking a shower, and then we're going to TS Jenison and we're knocking down that wall. Understood?"

"Is it my turn?" Dane said. "What happens if I say no?"

As Rhys made his way for the shower, he said over his shoulder, "You'll end up in a coffin at the bottom of the ocean."

Dane laughed as Rhys shut the door behind him. They both knew he wasn't joking.

CHAPTER 10

EMERY

TS JENISON WAS EMPTY AGAIN, AND EMERY WAS ALONE ON THE fifth floor, experiencing a heavy sense of déjà vu.

She wasn't even sure how she made it through the day, let alone the night.

After she arrived home and shut and locked the door behind her, she'd lay on her bed for hours staring at the ceiling, trying to make sense of what had happened with Rhys.

She kept circling back to the thought that maybe she'd imagined it.

It had to be the only explanation. Her daydreams were now so vivid that they seemed real.

Her mother would be proud of her.

Now Emery was in the maze of cubicles facing her office, trying to recreate what had happened. She'd been in the middle of the office when she'd been hauled clear across the room in the blink of an eye.

When she was alongside the cubicle that belonged to a

woman named Judith, Emery stopped to assess the distances. This looked about right.

She started walking and counted her steps.

By the time she reached the other side of the office where Rhys had pinned her against the wall, she'd counted to 349.

How the hell had he yanked her 349 feet in mere seconds?

It didn't make any sense.

"Losing my mind for sure." Emery went to her office and dropped into her desk chair. Head hung back, she lazily turned a circle using the toe of her ballet flat to push off the floor.

Maybe she'd been losing her mind all along. It would explain hearing people's thoughts. What if they were just random voices in her head? Hallucinations? When she'd first told her mother about them when she was just five years old, her mother had told her never to speak of it again.

It was the only time Emery's mom had ever portrayed equal parts anger and fear.

So maybe she'd been afraid Emery was crazy, and if she talked about it, she'd be admitted to a mental institution?

The Blake women certainly were cursed with bad luck.

Her own mother had died a little over six years ago when a bridge collapsed just outside of Saint Sabine. Her car had plummeted to the ravine down below, and her mom died on impact.

To this day, Emery still had trouble crossing bridges.

And before Emery was born, her grandmother died after being struck by lightning.

So maybe it wasn't so farfetched to believe Emery was suffering from a mental breakdown. It was the Blake curse coming to get her once and for all.

Maybe Emery should check herself into a mental institution.

Doctor: What brings you here today?

Emery: Well, I hear people's thoughts and I think I met a vampire.

Vampire.

It *was* crazy.

Emery pulled out a sheet of paper and wrote THINGS I KNOW ABOUT RHYS ROMAN at the top. Then below that, she started a list.

1. Incredible speed.

2. Fangs.

3. His eyes glowed

Emery tapped the pen against her chin as she thought. Three facts weren't damning, exactly—

Oh crap.

4. Came to the office after sunset.

Now if only she'd greeted him with a chunk of garlic around her neck. His garlic repulsion could have been the proof she'd needed!

Emery laughed to herself and leaned back again as she read over her notes. Maybe she needed a third party, someone neutral, someone to tell her she was being stupid.

Plucking her cell phone from her desk, she hit Morgan's name in her favorites list.

Morgan's face popped up on the screen. "Hi."

Emery dove right in. "Remember that time we went to that bonfire out at Hemlock's farm? And that girl...I don't remember her name...she told us that story about vampires?"

Morgan said, "Yes. The girl's name was Gabrielle. What about it?"

"Did you believe her?"

"Like do I believe vampires are real?"

Emery winced. It sounded even worse when some else said it, but maybe this was exactly what she needed—a cold splash of reality. "Yes. Vampires."

Morgan licked her fingers. A bag crumpled outside of the phone's camera. "I was the kid who put out a bowl of warm milk for the fairies," she said. "I might not be dressing in leather and fishnet stockings and gluing fake fangs to my teeth, but I don't *not* believe in vampires. I just haven't been given sufficient evidence yet.

"If I had the chance to meet a vampire, I would hands down take it. Why are you asking?"

Emery closed her eyes and kept spinning in her chair. Morgan wouldn't judge her, no matter how crazy she sounded. "Either Rhys Roman is a vampire or I'm going crazy."

Morgan got closer to the phone. "No fucking way. You know, now that you say it, I can see it."

Emery laughed. "Really? I'm glad one of us isn't totally freaking out about this."

"Tell me all of the details. Everything."

So Emery did. Everything minus the part where Rhys attacked her. Or...well, flew her across the room and then put his hands on her throat. She wasn't sure why she left that part out. Was it to protect Rhys?

Morgan said, "Let's say he *is* a vampire, why would he want to come to TS Jenison? Vampires are supposed to have everything because of the whole immortality thing, which explains him being a billionaire, now that I think about it. So what would he stand to gain from coming to the office?"

Emery gave herself another push in the chair. The base squeaked beneath her. "I don't know. He seemed awfully interested in the basement."

"Maybe he buried someone in the cement a hundred years ago like Chicago Mafia style."

Emery laughed, grateful for Morgan's levity. If she got nothing else out of this conversation, that would be enough. "I should probably go," Emery said when she realized the sun had already set. If she was really going to believe in vampires, then she should try not to be out after dark.

She'd stayed late to analyze what had happened the night before without the office staff being witness to her being ludicrous. But now that seemed like a mistake on her part. If Rhys wanted to find her again, TS Jenison after dark was a good place to come looking.

"When are you gonna see Rhys again?" Morgan asked. "Or are you going to call a vampire slayer and have him staked?"

"Hopefully never. And how do you even find a slayer?"

"Internet search, I bet. Maybe we should do a vampire sting. We can pretend we're the Coreys from *The Lost Boys*."

Emery slung her bag over her shoulder and clicked off the overhead light in her office. "I have enough on my plate, let alone adding *slay billionaire vampire* to it."

Morgan laughed out loud. "That's a problem I will gladly take from you."

"I'll call you later, okay?"

They said goodbye, and Emery climbed into the elevator, hitting the button for the ground floor. She'd made a point to park across the street today so that she'd be in clear shot of the lobby and the security guard just in case.

Except, when the elevator doors slid open, Emery realized how useless that had been.

Because Rhys was standing in the lobby, and this time, he hadn't come alone.

CHAPTER 11

EMERY

"Shit. Shit shit shit." Emery punched at the door button. Rhys took a step toward her. "No!" she shouted. "Stay back."

Rhys took another step. "Ms. Blake, wait—"

"Close goddammit!"

Suddenly, Rhys was in the elevator with her, his tall figure, broad shoulders, and overwhelming him-ness made Emery backtrack and slam into the wall.

If only she had a cross on her or some holy water!

"Back!" She dug in her purse and pulled out the first thing her hand touched—a ballpoint pen. "Or I'll stab you!"

Rhys scowled at her. "A ball point pen will do nothing."

"I bet it could take out an eye," she said, which she wasn't absolutely sure about. How much force would it take to stab a vampire in the eye? Did it at all compare to stabbing a fork through an olive? Because she could manage that. Also, gross.

Emery clutched the pen in her fist and cocked it back like a pick. "I'm not afraid to use this."

Rhys's hand snapped out and batted the pen from her grasp like it was a limp French fry.

"Hey!"

He grabbed her by the arm and steered her out of the elevator.

"This the one?" a tall, dark-haired guy said as he looked Emery up and down. The guy had a cocky tilt to his mouth, like he was two seconds away from either wolf whistling her or devouring her.

"What *one*?" Emery asked.

Rhys deposited her at the security desk. The night guard, Lori, sat in her swivel chair unblinking. "Lori? Are you okay?"

Lori didn't acknowledge her. She didn't even blink. And her head was absolutely blank.

Come to think of it, Emery couldn't hear anyone's thoughts.

"What did you do to her?" Emery asked. "Did you drug her?"

"She'll be fine," Rhys growled.

A woman with plump red lips and sharp black brows pushed a loose strand of hair behind Lori's ear. "She's just enthralled," the woman said. "It doesn't hurt. Usually."

"Enthralled?" Emery parroted.

"We can call it a mind drug, little girl," the dark-haired guy said. He got in close to her, overwhelming her. "I can try it on you if you'd like."

From behind him, Rhys let out a warning growl. The dark-haired guy frowned, a questioning look in his gaze. "What is it about you that has Rhys turned inside out, huh?"

Emery swallowed hard and licked her lips.

What did that mean?

She stole a look at Rhys, but he was turned away, hand in his hair.

Turned him inside out how? What had *she* done to him?

"What are you guys doing here? What do you want?"

"The little girl is bold," the dark-haired one said.

"Shut up, Dane," the woman said. "It's a pleasure to meet you, Emery. I'm Kat. This is Dane, and you've met Rhys. We're here looking for something, and maybe you can help us find it."

Emery narrowed her eyes at Rhys. "So you *were* looking for something last night? Meeting with me was just the cover."

She crossed the lobby until she was standing at Rhys's back, finger pointed at him. She wasn't sure where this bravado was coming from, but she wasn't about to question it now. She did not want the big scary, extremely good-looking possible vampire to know that she was afraid of him.

"Did you drag me into some kind of ploy? Are you trying to steal secrets from Tanner?"

Rhys turned back to her, laughing. But the sound was cold and dark. "I assure you, whatever secrets Tanner Jenison has, I have no desire to possess them."

"Then what is it? You want to raid our supply closet? You running out of sticky notes or something?"

Kat snorted. Dane, voice low, said, "Well, maybe I like this one."

"She is feisty," Kat said.

"A grand says she has Rhys bowing at her feet within a week."

"You're on."

Emery heard the telltale sound of two hands shaking on

a deal, but she wasn't going to get distracted by their games or the delicious thought of Rhys bowing anywhere near her.

"Then what are you doing here?" she asked Rhys.

He put his hands on his hips and inhaled wearily. "I need to get inside that tunnel."

She reeled back. Well...that's not what she thought he'd say.

"Why?"

"Because I have a problem, and I think my solution might be found there."

"What kind of problem?"

"A big problem."

"Oh okay. This is what we're doing. A big problem. What color is it? Brown? Purple? Does it hang high or low? Maybe you mean—"

Rhys hunched forward so his eyes were level with hers. He was inches away. His breath smelled of mint and something earthier.

His eyes bled to that impossible shade of blue, and though she had only known him two days, she was already clued in to the fact that when his eyes did that, danger followed.

Eyes didn't just change color and glow.

Humans couldn't cross a room in a blur.

And humans certainly couldn't mind control other humans.

The moment Emery realized just how real this was, her body went numb and a cool chill raced down her spine.

Vampire.

He was a vampire.

Vampires were real.

Someday soon, Emery was going to have to really confront that fact and pretty much relearn everything she thought she knew about the world. But right now, when a vampire was staring her down with his supernatural murder eyes? Definitely not the time.

Realizing she wasn't going to get him to budge, she said, "Okay fine. Good luck with your problem. I gotta go."

She started for the door. Rhys grabbed her wrist and swung her around so fast, she felt like she was on a carnival ride.

"No, you don't," he said. "You're coming with me."

"*What*? Why?"

Dane joined their side. "Because he thinks you're part of the prognostication."

"The what?"

"Prediction," Kat filled in as her heels clacked over the marble floor behind them.

"Prediction about what?"

"We can just enthrall her," Dane said. "Her questions are becoming tedious."

"I'm sorry I have a lot of questions about the vampires breaking into the basement of my place of employment."

Dane tsk-tsked. "So you think you have us figured out, do you?" To Rhys he said, "You didn't tell us she knew what we were."

Rhys said nothing.

"I'm not a vampire," Kat cut in.

"Oh. I'm sorry?" Emery said.

"No apologies necessary. I'm a witch."

Emery swallowed, blinked. "So...vampires and witches—"

"Are real. Yes yes. Let's move on," Dane said.

Now that they were in the stairwell, their voices echoed through the open space. Emery let her hand trail along the cool metal banister. Her touch was the only way she could be sure she wasn't dreaming.

"What else don't I know about the city I thought I loved so much?"

Dane frowned at her. "Can you not love a city with vampires? Honestly, little girl. We've been here longer than you. Rhys, please let's enthrall her."

"I'm not enthralling her," Rhys argued.

"It would solve all our problems," Dane said.

"I'm not fucking enthralling her."

Was the slightly dangerous, sorta scary, but also hot vampire seriously defending her?

Maybe Rhys wasn't as bad as she thought? Maybe if she just used some of her charm, maybe she could talk her way out of this futile mission. Except the words that came out of her mouth next were about as delicate as a hammer. "I really don't want to do this."

"See," Dane said, "the little girl doesn't want to be here. She's going to fight us the whole way."

"Stop calling me little girl," she shot back.

Dane's attention turned warm and amusing when he looked at her next. "You're what, twenty-three? Twenty-four?"

"Twenty-five," she corrected, feeling proud of that.

"I'm over five hundred years older than that. To me, you're practically a zygote."

"Five...hundred...."

Five...

Hundred...

Years old?

Just the thought of that many years centered a heavy weight on Emery's sternum.

That would mean...

Dane was around during the Middle Ages, the French Revolution, and King Henry VIII's reign.

Her brain couldn't even compute what that must be like. Even for an amateur history buff like herself, sometimes the stories she read in history books seemed like fiction because her modern brain had no frame of reference for a medieval world.

Dane had lived it.

"What about Rhys?" she asked. "How old is he?"

"Rhys doesn't talk about his age," Dane said.

"Why not?"

"Because he's old and crotchety."

"Is he older than you?"

Dane's expression could be likened to the same expression a child might give when a parent asked if they ate the last cookie...while the last cookie was smeared all over their face.

Rhys was older than five hundred years?

Emery was dizzy with this information. There was no way she could outsmart someone who'd lived over five hundred years. Knowing this, knowing what she was dealing with now, she realized facing off against Rhys was the same thing as playing checkers against a world champion chess player.

Basically, she was screwed. The only thing she could do now was play her part.

When they reached the lowest level, Rhys pushed through the basement's access door. It spilled out into the same hallway as the elevator, so they stood directly across from the entrance to the old tunnel.

Rhys went down the length of the tunnel and put his ear to the brick.

"What is he listening to?" Emery asked.

Dane leaned toward her. "Bricks speak a special language. He's listening to their frequency."

"Really?"

Dane smiled at her.

Kat said, "Don't be an ass."

Dane laughed.

Emery sighed. "Very funny."

"Shhh," Rhys chided.

They all went silent. Emery tried not to fidget as she stood between the impressively tall, gorgeous Kat and the broad-shouldered, impressively arrogant Dane.

After a handful of seconds, Rhys pushed away from the brick wall. "There's something back there."

"Really?" Dane crossed the hall. "Like what?"

"Something with a pulse. Not human. Energy."

"Ravenwood?" Kat asked.

"Raven what?" Emery said.

They all looked at her like she was a pony that had just begged for a carrot.

"It's a witch family name," Kat answered.

A weird feeling came over Emery. A witch family name?

Wood. Ravenwood. Witches and magic.

Maybe she was having a mental breakdown.

Dane turned to Rhys. "So how do you want to do this?"

Both men stood at the end of the hall, examining the brick. Neither of them had brought tools with, and it wasn't like TS Jenison had sledgehammers just lying around.

Rhys stepped up to the bricked archway and tightened his hands into fists.

Emery snorted. What, was he just going to punch his way through or—

Oh. Yup. That's exactly what he meant to do.

His first punch crumbled several bricks. On his second punch, he'd already made a hole through the wall.

Emery's heart kicked up. Okay maybe this was exciting. The hole Rhys had punched looked as though it led to an opening, not a caved-in tunnel. Any number of treasures could be back there.

She stepped closer, and Kat followed her.

"What do you see?" Dane asked when Rhys peered through the opening.

"Something glowing."

"Careful," Kat warned. "If it's magic, no telling how volatile it is."

Rhys looked at her over his shoulder. "That's why you're here, isn't it?"

A new chill had crept from the tunnel's opening, and Emery ran her hands up and down her arms to dispel the goosebumps. A shiver wracked her shoulders.

Trying to distract herself, she asked Kat, "So if you're a witch, what's your witchy family name?"

"Mine is Redheart."

"That does sound witchy."

Kat nodded, pride glinting in her eyes. "The Redheart line has a talent for power over the body. We're also immortal." She ran her hands appreciatively over her curves, and while it would have seemed conceited on any other woman, on Kat, Emery had to admit it was warranted. The woman was gorgeous.

"How many witch lines are there?" Emery asked.

Kat said, "In the beginning there were six."

"In the beginning? What does that mean?"

"Fables," Rhys muttered.

Kat frowned at him.

"Rhys doesn't believe in our origin stories," Dane said with a grin.

"Well, I definitely want to hear this now," Emery said.

Rhys huffed and continued pummeling the brick.

"It's said that all supernatural beings—vampires, witches, ghouls, demons, shifters, etc—came from Alius, the original world of the supernatural and magic," Kat explained.

Emery tried not to get hung up on all the rest of the creatures mentioned.

Demons. Ghouls? Shifters!

Vampires were apparently just the tip of the iceberg.

"So in the beginning," Kat said, "it's said that six witch families came to this world, but that was so long ago, and humans have entered the blood line so many times that now it's impossible to count how many lines there are."

Rhys stepped back, hands on his hips. "Your turn," he said to Dane, and Dane took up Rhys's spot at the widening hole.

"You can tell which line you are by the magic you carry though," Rhys said, still breathing heavily.

"True." Kat crossed her arms over her chest. "There's magic of the body. Elemental magic. The Thorns were good at mental magic. Then there's what we now call green witches, witches who are really good at manipulating and using nature."

This was all very fascinating, but Emery couldn't get past the idea that there was another world out there.

"So Alius...why is it just a fable? No one has been there?"

Rhys swiped his hair back with the rake of his fingers. "*If it ever existed, its gates have been closed for a very long time.*"

"And we should probably be thankful for that," Kat said to Emery.

"Why?"

"Because it's ruled by the Demon King."

"Allegedly," Rhys added.

"Ooooh tell me more." Emery did love a good fantasy tale.

Kat waved her hand in Rhys's general direction. "You think he's gorgeous and intimidating? Rhys would be a lowly peasant next to the Demon King."

"I take offense to that," Rhys said with a grumble.

Emery couldn't wrap her head around someone more intimidating (and gorgeous) than Rhys.

Dane stepped back from a hole big enough to walk through. Sweat beaded on his forehead. Vampires could sweat? Emery was learning so much about the undead.

Wait...were they undead?

There were too many interesting things to learn! She didn't even know where to start.

"So how do you open a gate anyway?" Emery asked. Might as well start with the most important bit. A demon king and an entire world of supernatural beings? That was something pretty significant.

"You need a traveler," Dane answered.

"Allegedly," Rhys said again.

"What's that?" Emery asked.

"Who the fuck knows," Dane said. He wiped the sweat away with the back of his shirt sleeve. "I do tend to side with Rhys on this one. No one has ever met a traveler. No one alive has ever been able to claim they've been to Alius. And we are supernatural, and a lot of us are immortal. You'd think someone would know something concrete."

Rhys stepped to the tunnel's opening. Cold air ghosted from the darkened space.

Dark save for a faint glow at the far end.

Goosebumps rippled down Emery's arms.

"So...are you here looking for a gate or a traveler or something?" she asked. Even though Rhys scoffed at every mention of the other world, why else would they be pummeling a bricked-up tunnel? This felt like a treasure hunt, and a gate to another world would be a boon.

Also...that probably wouldn't be good for *this* world.

Dane snorted. "We don't go looking for fables. We're here because—"

Rhys sent him a scathing look, and Dane cut himself off.

"What?" Emery said. "I can't know?"

"You'll know when you're supposed to know," Rhys answered with a fair amount of superiority.

She scowled at him. "I didn't even want to come down here."

"But we do enjoy your company," Dane said.

"I detect sarcasm," Emery said.

Dane slung his arm around Emery's shoulders. "Sarcasm? Noooo. Never."

"Dane," Rhys said, a growl rumbling in his chest.

Dane immediately pulled away from Emery. "My apologies," he said to Emery, and that time it sounded sincere.

"Let's focus on the task at hand," Kat said at the tunnel's opening. "You smell that? Like licorice root and roses."

Rhys stepped up beside her. "Ravenwood magic."

"Mmmm." Kat curled a hand around her hipbone. "Old too. I haven't smelled Ravenwood magic quite that pure in a long time."

Emery edged closer to the tunnel.

The chill in the air had dissipated, and now she was

flush, blood pooling in her cheeks. "So what is down there that's glowing?"

"Some kind of witch artifact, I'd guess," Kat answered.

"How powerful is it?" Rhys asked.

"This doesn't feel right," Dane said.

"I think we should take a closer look—"

Emery stepped through the opening in the brick wall.

"Emery!" Rhys shouted.

The ground shook, and the air popped. Emery whirled around to see Rhys lying on the floor all the way back by the elevators. Something had thrown him back.

"Holy shit," Dane said. "What the fuck was that?"

Emery hovered in the pool of light spilling through the opening in the wall. But there was something tugging on her, pulling her into the darkness.

"It's a barrier," Kat said as she reached her hand through. The air snapped at her, but didn't throw her like Rhys. She hissed and shook out her fingers. "God damn, that stung."

Dane took a tentative step and peered inside. "How come the little poppet can cross over?"

Rhys rejoined them. "Must be tuned to keep supernaturals out." He lifted his chin at Kat. "How long would it take you to remove the barrier?"

She made a pffft sound with her bright red lips. "Years maybe. Decades. Maybe never and then—"

Their voices faded away as Emery turned back to the glowing object.

"Emery!"

Emery blinked and looked over her shoulder. "Huh?"

"Are you all right?" Rhys asked, quieter now. He stood at the opening, eyes narrowed in panic. "I've been saying your name for a full minute."

"Oh. Sorry. Yeah. Totally fine."

"How do you feel about retrieving that artifact at the other end of the tunnel?"

"Well, hold on—" Kat said, but Rhys silenced her with a look.

"I can probably do that." Emery turned to the darkness and the glowing object at the other end.

There was an unmistakable tug at her core.

If she went to the end of the tunnel and grabbed the glowing object...if she could help Rhys...maybe he'd rethink making a deal on his land.

And then she could go back to her normal life and pretend none of this ever happened.

Was that what she wanted?

Of course it was.

Normal was good. Normal was...normal.

She stepped over some of the brick rubble. The darkness swallowed her up. Cobwebs hung from the ceiling and brushed against her hair. She barely noticed.

The closer she got to the object, the more intense the pulsing light, and when she came within reach of it, she realized it was floating in mid-air.

"What do you see?" Rhys called, his voice echoing around her down the tunnel.

Emery scrutinized the object. "It looks like a necklace."

It was distinctly circular, but there was no clasp.

"Can you describe it to me?" Kat asked.

"Umm...well..." Emery got closer, her face coming within the pool of glowing red light. The licorice scent was stronger now, and it tickled at her nose. It made her yearn for something she couldn't name. "Roped silver maybe? It's delicate. And there's a giant medallion at its center. Looks like weird letters have been inscribed inside the stone maybe? I don't know. I can't really make it out."

"Emery," Kat yelled. "I need you to get—"

Emery reached out for the medallion, and a wave of euphoria washed over her.

Their voices disappeared.

There was a rightness burning through Emery's veins. It was the same feeling she got when she came home from a business trip and finally got to sleep in her own bed back when she'd had a bed to call her own in an apartment that was all hers.

The pulsing light was warm on her skin.

Emery closed her hand around the medallion. All the air rushed out of her lungs as the light shot outward like a ripple in a pond. The ground trembled. Fire raced through Emery's body and circled her neck, sinking into her chest.

A shockwave reverberated back to her, shaking the ground beneath her.

Someone was shouting.

Energy pulsed in Emery's sternum as honeyed warmth spread through her veins...right before the light went out, and the darkness swallowed her up.

CHAPTER 12

RHYS

When Emery collapsed and the light was snuffed out, panic gripped Rhys. He surged for the tunnel, but Dane caught him around the chest and hauled him back. Rhys looked over at his second-in-command, rage burning in his gaze.

"You forget about the barrier?" Dane said.

Rhys growled. Yes, he had. Was the curse starting to affect his reasoning too? "How do we get her out?"

Kat frowned. "None of us are getting in there any time soon."

From outside the tunnel, Rhys could hear Emery's heartbeat. It was slow, but at least it was still beating.

"Emery!" he called, his voice bouncing around the tunnel. "Emery, can you hear me? Fuck." He turned to Dane. "Go get the first human you can find."

Dane nodded and was gone, the stairwell door clicking closed behind him.

Rhys ran a hand through his hair. He shouldn't have

forced Emery down here. What the fuck was he thinking anyway? His greed had prevailed. He wanted whatever the key was, and he wanted it now. And he'd put Emery in danger to get to it.

But what the fuck did he care what happened to a mortal girl? He barely knew her.

Breaking the curse was the only thing that mattered. The entire city depended on him figuring this shit out.

"Rhys," Kat said, "we should talk about what—"

Dane returned with the janitor, enthralled and complicit and slung over Dane's shoulder.

"Harry," Rhys said, a little relieved that the face was familiar. "I need you to go down that tunnel and bring Emery back to me."

Harry, eyes distant and heavy, looked at the hole in the wall. Rhys's impatience grew. He shoved the man through the opening, and the barrier let him through without complaint.

Using the flashlight on his cell phone, Harry shuffled down the tunnel. Rhys paced. Sometimes mortal speed was insufferable.

"Hurry, Harry," Rhys said.

Rhys could feel Kat and Dane having a silent conversation behind him. There was no telling what this Ravenwood medallion had done to Emery, or what the consequences would be. Usually, he was more strategic about the moves he made. For some reason, Emery seemed to make him wild and impulsive.

Or maybe that's just the curse breathing down your neck.

Rhys wasn't the glass-half-full kind of man. The Oracle had said the cure for the curse was at TS Jenison and that the girl factored into it. But Emery stumbling into a bricked-up tunnel and taking a magical medallion couldn't be the end of it. Breaking a curse that old and that powerful wouldn't be that easy.

And once upon a time, he'd known the Ravenwood witches well. They had always loved irony and revenge. There had to be more to this. Rhys could feel it.

Which meant they might have stumbled into worse problems.

Harry grunted as he lifted Emery into his arms. His mortal joints popped. The journey from the end of the tunnel back into the basement took so fucking long, Rhys was ready to punch through another brick wall.

"Will you calm down?" Kat said. "You're making me itchy."

Rhys growled at her. She just scowled at him.

Harry slowly made his way into the patch of light.

"What's got you bent out of shape anyway?" Dane asked. "Is it the glowing object or the little poppet that has you on edge?"

Good fucking question. And not one Rhys planned on answering.

When Harry finally stepped through to their side, Rhys took Emery from him and cradled her against his chest. Her coloring was pale, and her lips had lost some of their pinkness too. But other than that, she seemed all right.

"Was she carrying anything?" Kat asked the janitor. "Did you see anything on the floor maybe?"

Harry, still enthralled, stupidly shook his head.

Dane exhaled with exasperation. "Look." He pulled at the collar of Emery's blouse revealing what looked like a tattoo.

It went completely around her, connecting at the base of her neck. Roped threads that ended at a medallion just above her breasts.

Runes dotted the medallion's center.

"Fuck," he said beneath his breath.

He knew what that was. He knew what it meant.

"This is what I was trying to tell you," Kat said.

"Come on." Rhys started for the stairs. "I'm taking her back to the house. We can figure out the rest there."

"You think that's such a good idea considering what—"

Rhys rounded on Dane. His pupils blew out. His eyes were likely glowing with rage. He hated being questioned. He hated having to stop to explain himself to Dane of all people.

"Yes, I'm fucking sure," he said, his voice low and animal-like. "If you have any qualms about it, you can fucking leave."

Dane stepped back. Most of the time he didn't care about the hierarchy, and he'd fight Rhys until both of them were bloodied or temporarily dead.

But something on Rhys's face must have clued him in tonight.

Maybe it was the rumble in Rhys's voice. Or the bright glow of Rhys's eyes.

Or maybe it was the possessive way he held Emery to his chest, despite the necklace, despite everything.

No one would pry her from his grip. Not even Dane.

"Okay," Dane said. "I got it. The poppet stays."

Rhys turned for the stairs, flew up the stairwell, and raced for home, Emery held tightly in his arms.

CHAPTER 13

EMERY

Emery stretched her toes beneath the blanket and arched her back.

Damn, her sheets were really soft this morning. Did she change her fabric softener or something? It was like being nestled in a cloud. It'd been forever since she woke up feeling rested and comfortable and—

She's awake.

Emery jolted upright. Who the hell was in her room?

She looked around and realized she didn't recognize where she was. Panic kicked up in her chest.

Where was she?

The bed was a modern black iron bed with a dark gray duvet. The sheets were white and smelled freshly bleached, with a hint of lavender from the detergent.

Emery pulled herself up against the headboard to get a better look.

Moonlight stole through a bank of windows to her left. There was a cold fireplace directly across from the bed with a low settee in front of it. There were no lamps on in the room. Nothing to help her locate the person whose thoughts she'd just heard.

Tossing the duvet back, Emery put her feet to the floor, the plush threads of a thick rug squishing between her toes.

"Slow down," Rhys said.

She's all right, he thought. *So long as she obeys me and doesn't overdo it.*

Emery snorted. "Is this some kind of male chauvinistic thing you do?"

A lamp flickered on, and Rhys appeared on the other side of the bed. "You were knocked unconscious," he said. "I only suggested you not stand upright for your sake. If you suffered a concussion, you'll want to take it slow."

Knocked unconscious?

The last thing Emery remembered was being in the tunnel and....

The glowing necklace. She'd grabbed it hadn't she?

Can't tell her about the mark yet.

"What mark?"

"What did you say?" Rhys asked.

Wait...she could hear Rhys's thoughts?!

Relief flooded her. Not because she'd wanted to hear inside his head, exactly, but because she was worried her power had somehow been broken. How odd it was, that for most of her life she wished she could be rid of the ability, but as soon as it didn't work on someone, she was left flustered and annoyed by its absence.

Truth was, hearing thoughts was just who she was. Not being able to reach for that ability when she needed it felt like being blind.

"Mark," she repeated. "You said not to tell me about it. What mark?"

He hovered by her bedside, a deep frown on his sexy-as-hell face. Even rumpled and clearly anxious about something, he was ridiculously gorgeous. His hair was raked back from his forehead like he'd been running his hands through it repeatedly. There were bags beneath his eyes and his complexion looked paler than normal.

"How did you—you can *read my mind.*"

It wasn't a question.

He sounded a little aghast by the notion. Clear lines of tension settled into his body.

If she can read minds—fuck. Fucking hell. Don't think about last night.

Emery got a quick flicker of Rhys's fantasy from the office. Her bent over a desk, skirt shoved up to her waist, Rhys fucking her hard.

Followed by his teeth sinking into her flesh.

"Holy shit!" She leapt out of the bed, flush and immediately turned on.

What the hell was wrong with her? *That* turned her on? Him fucking and biting her?

Yeah, it really did. Like really *really* turned her on. And judging by the sudden molten stare coming from Rhys, he could sense it too.

"Sorry," she said with a wince. "I've always been able to read minds. But when I met you, there was nothing. I haven't heard a single one of your thoughts. Until now."

Rhys paced away, hands on his hips. "Always?" he said. "For as long as you can remember?"

"My first clear memory of reading someone's thoughts was from my 5th birthday when my *now former* best friend thought, 'Emery's a stupid doo-doo head.' Still working through that blow."

Rhys turned back to her, fresh amusement replacing his earlier agitation.

Emery couldn't help it, she smirked too.

It *was* a funny story.

"But now…" Rhys trailed off.

"Now I can hear your thoughts."

Her cheeks flamed again when her filthy dirty mind pulled up a replay of him bending her over a desk.

That image was going to be burned in her head until the end of time.

Did he want to do that to her? Like did he actually find her attractive? Or was it just like a power play thing? Or maybe a vampire power play thing?

Maybe the better question was, if he offered to bend her over a desk, would she take him up on that offer?

Yes.

No!

Yes, you would.

Rhys dropped onto the settee and put his elbows to his knees. "Can you hear my thoughts now?"

Emery zeroed in on him. She didn't usually have to think too hard to hear someone's thoughts, but his head was quiet again.

"Now? No. It seems like it's gone again."

He nodded and exhaled, a little relieved. "Most vampires can shield their mind if they know there's a need for it."

"Really?" Emery crossed the room. "Why would you have to? Were there others like me?"

"Yes."

"Okay now I'm definitely intrigued." She sat down beside him. Her leg was pressed against his, and it sent a deep thrill through her that pooled between her legs.

"Tell me more," she coaxed.

Rhys folded his hands and bowed his head. "That's a very long story."

"I have time."

"I don't."

"What does that mean?"

He tipped his head toward her, his gaze trained on her chest. "The mark you heard me thinking about."

She followed his line of sight and looked down at her chest. There was just a sliver of black ink peeking out from the collar of her shirt. "What the—" She pulled the collar down, then down further, until the whole tattoo was exposed. "How did that get there? Isn't that...that's the necklace. The necklace from the tunnel."

"It would seem so."

"But how did it become a tattoo? On my chest?"

"Magic"

"What does this mean?"

He looked over at her out of the corner of his eye. His lips were impossibly wet and impossibly close.

Was she leaning into him? Closer? Yup.

She liked the feel of him pressed against her.

"What do you know about your heritage?" he asked. "Your ancestors?"

Emery frowned at him. "Ummm...not much? My mom was an only child. My grandmother was dead before I was born. The men in our lives have always been absent, so I don't know much about my father or my grandfather."

Another one of the Blake women's curses, one that Emery had thought she'd escaped when she found Michael.

But lo and behold, the curse struck again!

"If you can read minds," Rhys said, "then there is some magic in your family lineage."

Emery laughed. "Magic? No way. Not possible."

But then she thought of the Wood family name and...

"No," she said again, more forcefully. "I'm definitely not magical."

"What do you call reading minds?"

Well, he certainly had a good point there.

"I think I need a drink," she said.

"You just fainted not four hours ago—"

She made her way for the door. Or what she thought was the door. "I need a drink, Rhys the Vampire, and while you might be fast and fangy, I don't think there's anything you could do to stop me from getting one."

He sighed, and when she pulled open a door to a bathroom, he said, "Very well. But you won't find one in there."

She turned back to him.

He nodded to a door beside the fireplace. "It's this one."

"Lead the way."

CHAPTER 14

EMERY

Rhys led Emery downstairs and to a huge room in the back of the house.

When they walked through the large arched doorway, Emery marveled at the lux architecture and furnishings. There were several sitting areas around the room and two massive stone fireplaces on either side, the mantles carved to resemble a lion's head.

Opposite the doorway was a bank of floor-to-ceiling windows that overlooked the back garden, and beyond that the moonlit harbor.

It was a gorgeous view that normally would have captured Emery's attention, except the room was full of people who she suspected were not *people* but vampires.

Walking into the parlor, she started to doubt her life choices. This felt like the beginning of a bad joke.

A mortal girl walks into a room full of vampires...

When Rhys came in behind her, the whole room went

silent. Emery could sense the shift in the air like a drop in the barometric pressure.

Emery had never been one to like being the center of attention. She'd do it if the job called for it, and sometimes her role as Tanner's assistant required it. But she'd be anxious days leading up to the event and exhausted for days afterward.

So standing at the head of the room with everyone's attention on her, Emery immediately wanted to retreat and curl into a safe corner. Not only because they were all looking at her, but because they were all as gorgeous as gods.

Kat was the first to step forward. "You're awake," she said to Emery. "I'm glad you're okay."

"Me too." Emery hovered by Rhys's side unsure of where her place was in this room.

She counted eleven other people here not including her, Rhys, and Kat.

Kat gestured to those gathered around the large leather sofas that sat closest to the doorway. "These are the sentinels of House Roman. If you spend any length of time here, you'll get to know their faces."

If she spent time here? Did she now have a standing invitation?

Tanner would flip if he learned about that. It was like having a standing invitation to Buckingham Palace.

"What are sentinels?" Emery asked.

Dane disentangled himself from two women on the sofa. "Sentinels are guards of the house and its reputation, and guards of the Turned."

The Turned. Other vampires. She could make that connection easily.

"Nice to meet you all," she said and gave an awkward wave.

They all nodded and said hello, then Rhys gave a quick flick of his hand, and they dispersed without question or objection.

That was impressive.

"Have a seat," Rhys said to her as he went to a bar along the room's far wall. Mirrors had been installed on the wall behind rows and rows of every kind of liquor under the sun. "What do you want to drink?"

"Gin and tonic."

"Classy little poppet," Dane said as he sat on one of the sofa's arms and propped his boot on the cushion. "Did we figure out—"

"Emery can read minds," Rhys said as he threw her drink together.

Emery didn't miss the way Dane and Kat looked at each other like there was more to that admission than just the facts stated.

But also, how refreshing was it that these people—supernatural beings—knew her deepest secret and didn't totally dismiss her? It was a bit of a relief after all of these years of keeping that to herself.

"She can read minds, can she?" Dane narrowed his eyes at Emery and then brought to mind an image of him having sex with one of the girls who'd just left the room.

"Oh gross!" Emery exclaimed and scrubbed at her eyes like that might drive away the image. "Stop that!"

Dane whistled. "Okay, I believe it."

Kat's thoughts echoed what actually came out of her mouth. "Don't be an asshole, Dane."

"Why stop now?" Dane said. "It comes so naturally."

When Rhys came over, drink in hand, he whacked Dane upside the back of the head. "Be respectful."

Dane looked a little annoyed, but not put out. "I absolutely will not."

"Kat," Rhys said. "May I speak with you privately?"

Kat made her way out of the room without so much as a question.

Rhys turned to Dane. "Emery is in your hands. Don't make me regret that decision."

Dane smiled over at her. "I'll take good care of her."

As Rhys disappeared through an arched doorway, Emery couldn't help but watch his retreating form, the way his broad shoulders nearly filled up the doorway, how the thin material of his t-shirt filled the hollows of muscle down his back.

Gods that man.

He might just be the death of Emery if she didn't get her shit together.

But now that he was gone, maybe she could take advantage of it.

Working in the corporate world, Emery had learned a thing or two about how to suss out information that could be used to her advantage. Rhys was clearly the one in charge here, but Emery was learning that Dane had the potential to be a loose cannon.

"Why were you guys looking for this thing—" Emery pointed at the tattoo "—in the basement of TS Jenison anyway?"

Emery sipped her drink and grumbled at the lack of gin. Rhys had obviously poured light.

Dane sat back and spread his arms over the sofa. "We weren't looking for the necklace, exactly, but a way to end the curse."

"Curse?" Butterflies woke in her belly. Now they were getting somewhere. She set the glass on the iron coffee table. "What curse is that?"

"The Ravenwood curse, of course. Did Rhys not tell you?"

She made a noncommittal face at him. Better not to answer that directly. "Is there some kind of grudge between Rhys and these Ravenwoods?"

"Oh, you sweet newborn baby."

She picked up the drink again. "I'm not sure I like you."

He laughed out loud. "As if I need the admiration of a—" He stopped himself and cut his gaze to hers. "Mortal," he finished, like he'd meant to say something else entirely.

"So...a curse, a prediction, witches and vampires." Emery drained the last of her glass, and being bold, decided to help herself to the liquor. Dane followed her over and folded his arms on the bar top. "You said Rhys thought I was part of the prediction. What was the prediction again?"

Dane tsk-tsked at her. "I see what you're doing, poppet."

Emery found the bottle of gin, nestled amongst several bottles of expensive vodka. "I don't know what you're talking about."

If only she hadn't opened her big mouth about being able to read minds, Dane and Rhys and Kat wouldn't know to shield their thoughts from her, and she could have really gotten to the bottom of this whole thing.

What she needed was Rhys's trust so she could secure his land and get the promotion.

But damn, had she overshot. Now she knew vampires were real, and a magical necklace had imprinted itself on her chest.

If she dwelled on those details too long, she might go mad.

"All you need to know as of right now," Dane said, "is that you're somehow holding the key to this damnable curse, which means you now have Rhys twisted around your little finger."

"Oh?" She raised a brow. She could work with that.

But Dane didn't see it as the boon she did.

There was still a hint of a smile on his face, but his voice took on a more sinister tone when he said, "Choose your next steps wisely, poppet. Got it?"

"Of course," she answered and went about pouring a drink.

She had to remember just who and what she was dealing with. Rhys wasn't just a reclusive billionaire.

He was a vampire. Several centuries old. And the leader of a house of vampires.

Like Little Red Riding Hood, she'd stumbled into the wrong dark forest.

From now on, she needed to be very, very careful.

Lest she be devoured by the big bad wolf.

CHAPTER 15

RHYS

Without his command, Kat went straight to his office and sat in one of the matching leather chairs in front of his massive oak desk.

"Okay, so Emery can read minds," she said as she folded one long leg over the other knee.

He shut the door behind them, and Kat waved her hand through the air, sealing the room from listening ears and prying eyes.

Rhys could immediately smell her magic, coppery and sweet.

"Does this mean what I think it means?" she said.

"What else could it mean?" He paced around the backside of his desk. He went to the giant circular window that overlooked the harbor across the street.

When he'd been forced from his home, this seemed like the next best place to put down roots. The land had still been untouched, but he knew being along a coastline would eventually pay off. For thousands of years, people had settled along waterways.

He'd been right of course. Now Second Quarter was one of the most lucrative sections of Saint Sabine, somewhat thanks to him. He'd built House Roman—the *second* House Roman—in the late 1700s. It now had one of the best views in Second Quarter.

Harbor lights glittered on the water. Yachts and sailboats bobbed in the marina, tied to their docks.

But Rhys wasn't seeing any of that.

He had bigger problems.

"I'm truly lost here," Kat said. The leather groaned as she readjusted in her chair. "How does Emery fit into a Ravenwood curse if she is what we think she is?"

Rhys turned back to the room. "I don't fucking know." He came around the desk and dropped into the chair beside Kat. He spread out his long body, the exhaustion creeping in.

"Maybe you should take her to Last Vale," Kat said quietly.

He turned his head to her. "Are you fucking joking?"

"Think about it. What do you have to lose?"

"Emery was already in danger once in that tunnel. Now you want me to take her to the curse?"

Rhys could feel Kat analyzing him in that way only she could. She might not have been around as long as Dane or Ramses, but Kat had always taken the time to know him better, and right now, he was not acting like himself.

"Why do you care what happens to the girl?" Kat asked.

And there it was.

He was centuries old. There were hundreds of bodies in his past.

Why would one girl matter at all?

"What if taking her there somehow makes it worse?" he argued. "We don't know what this means."

Kat spread out her arms. "Worse than this?"

She was making it difficult to argue with.

"Okay, fine." He got up. "But if this somehow goes sideways, I'm blaming you."

RHYS AND KAT returned to the parlor to find Dane and Emery in the middle of a game of billiards. Emery was laughing at something Dane said while Dane lined up a shot on one of the solids.

Seeing Dane be casual with Emery made Rhys feel oddly jealous.

The fuck was wrong with him?

"Emery," Rhys said. "I have something to show you."

Dane slid the pool cue across his knuckle, and the cue ball hit the red solid into the side pocket.

"We're in the middle of a game," Emery said.

"Don't worry, poppet," Dane said. "I would have won anyway."

She frowned over at him. Dane laughed.

Rhys growled. "Come."

Thankfully, she didn't fight the command, and Rhys led her out of the house.

"Where are we going?" she asked, trailing behind him. It wasn't as if he were using his vampiric speed.

"You want my land, Ms. Blake, but you don't fully understand what you're asking for, so it's time I finally showed you."

CHAPTER 16

Rhys was going to take her to the land?

Things were starting to look up.

She didn't care about the tattoo or the fact that vampires were real. Her work was real, and it was normal, and what she needed more than anything was to make a deal with Rhys Roman for that land.

They spilled onto the street and were swept up in the tide of late-night pedestrians and tourists.

Across the street, the same band at Glady's played a vibrant jazz tune. Emery was caught by the energy that moved between each member of the band, how their bodies swayed with the music while their fingers stroked the strings and the keys.

"I love the Second," she said wistfully as they waited at the next street corner for the traffic light to change.

Rhys looked down at her, his eyes catching and reflecting the golden glow of the old-fashioned street lamps.

"I do too. I've been here almost as long as I've been in America."

The light changed, and the crowd surged forward. Beside Emery, a couple, slightly inebriated, stumbled forward, laughing. A group of men up ahead were joking about one of their friends' recent dating faux pas.

If Emery lived in the Second, she'd be out here every night, walking with the crowds. There was so much energy and vibrancy. She'd liked the neighborhood where she and Michael had shared an apartment—it was safe enough and quiet—but the apartment buildings had once been housing for local factory workers back in the 1930s, and so the design was utilitarian, lacking in all things the Second had.

"How long have you been in America?" Emery asked.

"A little over three hundred years."

Three hundred years. It almost made Emery's head swim just trying to do the math, trying to piece together all of the things he might have witnessed in that time. The birth of the country, for one.

The Revolution. The Civil War.

"Did you know George Washington?" she asked because that was literally the first person that popped in her head.

An amused smile came over his kissable lips when he looked over at her. "I did, yes."

"Oh, tell me something interesting about him."

"He had horrible teeth, and even worse dentures."

Emery frowned. "That's not the insightful wisdom I wanted on our first president."

He stepped aside to let a group of rowdy men pass by as they jostled each other and laughed. "I find the personal details of historical figures the most fascinating."

"I suppose it does make him more human...wait, he *was* human, right?"

"Yes. The teeth proved it. But Abraham Lincoln on the other hand..." He trailed off as if he'd heard something Emery hadn't.

"Wait, what? Abraham Lincoln? What about him?"

Rhys held up his hand, and then a group of young boys came barreling around the corner, one slamming right into Rhys. Rhys caught the boy beneath the arms before he bounced back to the concrete.

When the kid looked up at Rhys, he laughed and said, "Shit, Rhys. Sorry man."

Rhys frowned. "Cussing becomes no man, Gabe."

Gabe rolled his eyes. Did he realize Rhys was a several-hundred-year-old vampire?

"Old man and his lessons," the kid said. "I've heard you swear before."

"I've earned it."

Gabe snorted. "So have I."

The others hung in a loose circle behind the boy, chatting and cajoling each other while they waited.

"Where were you headed?" Rhys asked.

"Ipsi's."

Rhys dug into his pocket.

Ipsi's was a vintage soda shop. Along with every malt and ice cream shake you could imagine, it also had an entire wall of candy to select from. Michael used to take Emery on occasion so she could stock up on their French salted caramels. She hadn't been there since their breakup. She braced for the inevitable pang of sadness that always came with a memory of what had been, but...she was surprised to find there was no heartache attached to it.

Rhys handed Gabe several twenty-dollar bills. "Buy me a box of the cordials and deliver it to the house. You can keep the rest."

The kid beamed. "I knew I liked you for a reason, old man."

"Mmhmmm." Rhys gave him a look that Emery could only describe as parentally exasperated.

She had to admit, this was a side of the immortal, extremely dangerous vampire she hadn't expected.

"Go on then." Rhys waved the kids away.

"See you!" The kids took off, running again. Now they had money to burn.

"Old man?" Emery said and tried to bury her laughter.

Rhys motioned them forward, and they crossed the intersection with a bustling group of pedestrians.

"Gabe is the son of one of our house staff. I let him get away with it because his mother is an excellent employee."

Emery looked up at him with a knowing smirk. "Oh right. I'm sure that's the reason."

There was a telltale smile trying to pull at the corner of his full mouth.

"So, Abraham Lincoln," she tried again.

Rhys just smiled and kept walking. "The night grows old, Ms. Blake. Come."

She'd just have to ask Kat or Dane later. They probably knew.

They kept walking south on Garden Street. Soon the crowd thinned, and the streets grew quieter. When the street curved east and went back uphill toward the city's business district, Rhys stopped.

They'd reached the parcel Tanner wanted to buy from Rhys. The stretch of land every businessperson in Saint Sabine salivated over.

While the sidewalk followed the curve of the street and went north, Rhys and Emery stood at the mouth of a dirt path tucked between two rose bushes. The path disappeared into the woods.

While the city's sounds had faded, the forest was alive with noise. Crickets and tree frogs and owls hooting in the night. In the distance, fireflies winked in the twilight.

The thought of someone bulldozing this place to build high-rises suddenly made Emery sick to her stomach.

Rhys looked down at her. There was a street lamp just behind him, the globe lit golden in the descending night. It rimmed him in hazy light, but shadowed his face. Emery couldn't make out his expression, and a flicker of fear winked on in her brain, alarm bells jangling.

She'd just watched him interact with a boy on the street and request cordials for a treat for later, but just two days ago, he'd had her pressed against the wall in the office of TS Jenison, his eyes flashing with a preternatural glow.

Now that she knew he was a vampire, she could look back and see that attack for what it was—hunger.

Rhys was a dangerous man.

And she was alone with him at the mouth of the forest.

"This way," he said and gestured to the path.

"In there?"

"Yes."

"Go into the dark woods with a several-hundred-year-old vampire," Emery said as she scanned the darkness. "What could possibly go wrong?"

Rhys edged closer, and his scent suddenly overwhelmed her. Something sweet and masculine, like amber and spice and leather. When he spoke, his voice was low and throaty. "I assure you, Ms. Blake, if I wanted to bite you, I would have done so by now." He reached out and pushed aside a lock of her hair exposing her neck. "And there's nothing that you could do to stop me."

Emery's heart spiked at his touch, and an answering thrill slithered down her belly, pooled between her legs. It didn't take long for her to feel the dampness in her panties.

What was wrong with her? Was she out of her damn mind?

She seriously needed to get her shit together.

"All right," she said, trying to portray calmness while her insides knotted and her nerves crackled and her clit throbbed.

She stepped through the rose bushes, and...it was like stepping into another world.

The air was thicker and humid, but cold too so that her bare arms were immediately covered in goosebumps.

Outside of the forest, the night had been pleasant and clear, but in here, mist hung in the air.

"Whoa. That...is weird."

"It gets weirder."

Seriously?

Rhys surged ahead on the path, and Emery had to jog to keep up with him.

The darkness grew thicker. Emery's human eyes weren't cut out for this, and when she tripped over a stick, her feet went out from beneath her.

Rhys was suddenly beside her, his hands on her waist. Emery sucked in a breath as he pulled her in closer, steadying her. Her pulse points drummed, though with exhilaration or fear, she couldn't tell.

"Are you all right?" Rhys asked.

For a split second, he dropped his mental guard on his thoughts, and all Emery could see was his fantasy of biting her, the blood running down his throat.

Just one bite, he thought. *One sweet, intoxicating bite.*

Emery lurched back. "I'm fine. Totally cool."

Rhys's concern vanished, and his expression hardened. "Come. We're almost there."

His tall, dark form disappeared into the mist, and Emery, heart racing and body pulsing, could only stumble behind.

CHAPTER 17

RHYS

Rhys wanted to give in to the madness.

Take Emery by the throat and sink his teeth into her flesh, taste her on his tongue.

And fantasizing about it turned him hard and restless. He wanted to fuck and bite her. Fuck her some more and listen to her moan beneath him.

He wanted to possess her.

Rhys had never been denied much since being Turned. And yet, he could not give in to this, to her.

He needed to clear his head if he was going to save his Turned and the city he loved.

They moved on through the forest, and when the light of the curse appeared over the next hill, tension rippled through Rhys's body.

They were almost there.

He reached the top of the hill first and waited for Emery to catch up, keeping careful attention on her footsteps.

He'd save her if he needed to, but if he got close to her again...

His cock was rock hard, and his fangs were threatening to come out. His control was razor thin. It took everything inside of him to keep him from throwing her on the forest floor and—

Emery joined him on the hill's crest.

Rhys focused on strengthening his mental shield. Was it working? He stole a glance at Emery. She was out of sorts still, but she didn't seem like she was getting a head full of his dark, twisted fantasies.

"Whoa," Emery said. "What is this?"

Rhys finally turned back to the valley down below.

For the first time in a long time, he could see the ghost town through someone else's eyes. It'd been too long since he'd returned.

Down below, sleepy and dark and shrouded in mist, was a ghost town.

His ghost town.

"This," he said, "is Last Vale."

CHAPTER 18

EMERY

THE MOONLIGHT HAD FINALLY STOLEN THROUGH WHATEVER magic this place possessed and shone down on thatched roofs and glittered off bubbled glass windows.

The town stretched at least a mile in every direction. It was no tiny outpost. There must have been a least two thousand people here when it was inhabited.

Emery hurried down the hill and through a narrow meadow that lay between the ghost town and the forest. She stumbled onto a dirt road, ruts still in the earth from old wagon wheels.

"How is this possible?" she said. "How is this right next to Saint Sabine, and no one has ever said anything about it?"

"Kat," he answered.

Emery passed a bakery and a library and a post office, her head twisting back and forth to take it all in.

"It's veiled on all sides with magic," Rhys went on, "so

even if you sail past from the ocean, it just looks like unin-habited woods."

"I am in awe," she said as she peered through the window of a milliner. Feathered hats were set out on iron stands in the window. There was paper stacked up on the counter and boxes ready to be filled on the shelves. It was like everyone just up and disappeared, a life trapped in amber.

When Emery stumbled back into the street, she read a sign over a three-story building that said, Last Vale Hotel.

"That's the town's name? Last Vale?"

Rhys nodded, the glow of the moonlight highlighting half his face. "It was one of the first settlements in the area, a popular port on the eastern seaboard."

"It's incredible."

The street turned around a corner, and when Emery turned with it, she came to a stop. Where the last street had been in pristine condition, this street looked like it'd seen a war.

There was a broken wagon lying on its side in the middle of the street with a giant skeleton of a horse.

One of the shops to the left had a hole torn in its wall like someone had crashed through it. Windows were broken and glass glittered on the street.

As Rhys came to a stop beside her and sighed, Emery looked over at him. "What happened?"

"Witches happened," he said. "Ravenwoods, specifically. There was a disagreement."

"I'll say."

"It was a rather large disagreement."

"Go on."

He sighed again and took a few steps forward. "Are you familiar with ley lines?"

"Aren't they like lines of energy or something that connect ancient structures like Stonehenge?"

"That's the modern pseudo-science definition. In truth, ley lines are a vein of power. And witches are particularly good at tapping into them." He stopped at the overturned wagon.

"So the disagreement...does that have anything to do with the curse?"

He turned back to her and frowned. "How do you know about the curse?

"Dane," she explained.

"Fucking hell," he said beneath his breath. "Well, I was getting to that part."

"I'm waiting."

He went to the horse and plucked a giant rib bone from the skeleton. "There's a ley line that runs through here." He gestured to the northwest. "The Ravenwood witches were of the opinion that they should own this land because of it. I was of the opinion that they were wrong."

Now it was starting to make sense.

"So they cursed you?"

He tossed the bone back to the skeleton where it crashed with several others, knocking them off the spine like bowling pins.

"Follow me," he said and surged forward again.

Emery hurried to follow. He took a right down a side street where the ocean lay at the other end. Sea spray came up, and when the wave crashed down again, it was almost like music, trickling between the rocks. The air smelled salty and crisp.

But before they reached the shore, Rhys turned left onto the next street and stopped in the intersection looking north.

Emery came up beside him a few seconds later, a little breathless and a little excited to uncover his secrets.

Until she followed his line of sight.

"Holy shit," she whispered.

On a hilltop overlooking the town and the ocean, sat an impressive mansion made of stone. A vibrant red light glowed inside, but outside, the house was covered in a wet, black film.

"That's my house," Rhys said. "And that's where the curse began."

CHAPTER 19

RHYS

As a vampire, Rhys rarely felt ill. But as he took Emery up the stone steps to his old house, the place where the curse originated, his stomach churned.

It'd been a long time since he'd returned to this place. Just being here was probably a mistake, for him and for Emery.

What if he lost himself here? What if something happened to Emery?

He could still hear Kat in the back of his head: *And why does it matter what happens to her?*

Why, indeed.

When they reached the top of the hill, they stopped to take in the sight of the house. Black ooze had started to weep from the stones the day after the curse was wrought. Now it covered the entire stone façade and had spread out to the earth too.

After he and Dane had cleaned up the mess following the confrontation with the Ravenwood family, Rhys thought it was the land that was cursed, and he vowed never to let another person touch it.

He made up a story about noxious fumes that were driving people mad, and he and Dane ordered everyone to move to what was now Second District.

The humans bought it and packed up. Thinking it was only temporary, they left most of their belongings.

As time went on, a new neighborhood was established. By that point, Kat's spell had done its job. Everyone forgot about Last Vale, and Rhys started to think the curse could be sealed inside the town, closed off like a tomb.

He'd grown lazy, thinking the problem had solved itself.

But in the last several years, Rhys's Turned had started to go mad.

There was an attack two months ago in an alley in the Second. The vampire, a man Rhys had turned in the 70s, had attacked a young woman he'd plucked off the street. The vampire had been punished, locked away in one of the cells beneath House Roman. Rhys had made the mistake of thinking the effects of the curse would come and go. He'd been wrong.

The vampire descended into total madness and eventually killed himself by smashing his head against a wall.

It seemed the older the vampire, the more immune they were, but if Rhys was starting to feel the effects...

He looked over at Emery, now bathed in the red glow of the curse. Her eyes were transfixed.

Could she really be the solution, and if so, how?

Could this *girl,* who came out of nowhere, really fix one of Rhys's biggest problems?

She's not just some girl.

That was true enough.

"What does the curse do?" Emery asked.

"The curse," he said, "seems to be turning me and mine into feral monsters."

"Ahh," she said, not at all shocked by it. He'd expected her to reel back at the very least.

"That's obviously a problem. So..." She looked around. "How do we stop this curse?"

"I've been trying to figure that out for centuries," he admitted. "But the Oracle—the prediction—suggested that you were a solution."

"Me?" she squeaked.

"Yes, you."

She frowned up at him. "That seems extremely unlikely."

"Does it?" He turned to face her. "The necklace on your chest says otherwise."

Her frown deepened. "Is that why you brought me here? Hoping I'd end the curse?"

Habit had him reaching for a lie.

For some reason, he wanted Emery to have the truth and make the decision for herself.

"Yes," he answered. "Though I don't know how we might go about it."

"Maybe we should go inside?"

"I suppose that's a good place to start." Except the very thought had a stone forming in his gut. Sweat beaded along his temple.

He reached his hand out for the iron door handle.

The black ooze had left the door mostly untouched. When he pushed the door in, the old hinges creaked and echoed through the cavernous space.

Though the outside of the house was covered in the ooze, the inside was untouched.

"Stay by my side," he told Emery before they entered.

"And don't touch anything until we're sure we know what it is."

"Copy that," she said and followed behind him through the front door.

The air was wet inside and smelled of licorice and roses. It brought back far too many memories that Rhys would rather stay buried. If he let his mind wander, he could still hear the sounds of that night, the night the battlelines had been drawn. The sound of crushed bones and the deep reverberation of a witch curse being born.

They went down the foyer, following the glowing pulse of the curse, with Rhys in the lead.

He knew where they were going. He knew where the root lay.

When they rounded into the long dining room, Emery gasped.

A giant energy source pulsed and throbbed in the air. It glowed so brightly at its center that Rhys had to shield his eyes. Wind shot around the room rattling the paintings on the wall.

Was it always like this?

Rhys couldn't remember.

It took him a second to realize Emery was shouting at him and gesturing at her chest.

The tattoo was glowing the same neon red as the curse.

He couldn't make out what Emery was saying. It was like they were facing a hurricane.

The curse point bloomed outward, several tendrils of energy snapping like a whip.

The air crackled as a tendril reached out for Emery.

Rhys tried to yank her back, but even with his vampire speed, he wasn't fast enough.

Emery gasped as the magic connected with the tattoo. Her hair lifted around her face and her feet left the ground.

"Rhys! What is happening?!" She stretched out for him, and when their hands connected, power roared through him. It was too much, and his skin stretched taut, threatened to break.

Rhys gritted his teeth, trying to hold himself together, but in an explosion of light and sound, the power threw him back, and he slammed against the wall.

The ground shook as a wave of energy pulsed out from Emery and rippled across the room. The hair lifted at the back of his neck as his vision dimmed.

The last thing Rhys saw was Emery mid-air glowing like a supernova.

CHAPTER 20

EMERY

When Emery opened her eyes, she was lying on a plush rug, her face mashed against the leg of a table. Her head was foggy.

"What the—" She sat up and scrubbed at her eyes. Using the table for support, she climbed to her feet and expected to be achy and sore. Usually, passing out on the floor wasn't good for the bones, but she felt surprisingly good. Like *really* good.

She looked around the massive dining room and remembered where she was—Rhy's house in Last Vale.

And it was like stepping back in time.

There were oil paintings in gilded frames hanging on the wall and furniture that seemed old, but also shockingly new. There was a vase in the center of the table, the flowers and foliage practically mummified.

Emery took a step around the table and saw someone lying on the floor.

"Rhys!" She crashed to her knees beside him and shook his shoulders. "Rhys, wake up!"

Should she check for a pulse? Did vampires even have a pulse?

"Rhys!"

He lurched awake, his eyes glowing angry blue.

Emery shimmed back on all fours.

"It's okay. It's just me," she said.

"Emery?" He blinked, and the glowing of his irises faded. "What—" He looked past her. "The curse."

God, she'd forgotten all about that!

She looked down and parted her shirt and found the necklace tattoo still on her skin. But it was no longer glowing. Good sign, hopefully?

"How do you feel?" Rhys asked.

Emery sat back on her butt. "Honestly? I feel fine."

Rhys helped her to her feet, but once she was up, he kept his arm around her shoulders and tucked her into his side. "You're sure you're all right?" he asked.

She smiled up at him. His hair was disheveled, and there was a permanent frown on his face. His concern for her was evident, and that made Emery feel warm and fuzzy inside.

Did he care about her or only about ending the curse?

Probably the latter. He barely knew Emery. And he was several hundred years old. Why should he care about her of all people?

Except his arm around her...it was awfully protective. And despite being a vampire, the line of his body beside her was cold, but comforting.

"I'm really okay," she said. "How do you feel? Any impending madness?"

He gave a short laugh. "So far I seem to be well."

"Good," he said, but the pinch between his brows said otherwise. "Come. You should get home and lie down."

Emery tried digging into his head, but his mental shields were firmly up.

Rhys pulled her down the wide foyer and out the front door.

Outside, some of the heavy darkness that hung over the town when they'd first arrived had faded. The moonlight shone brightly on the abandoned streets.

In the mansion's front yard, they turned to look back at the house.

The black ooze was gone.

Now the house stood proudly and strongly against the twilight sky.

"My God," Rhys said. "It really did work."

Emery clapped her hands together. "Yay!" she said like a big nerd. "We did it!"

Rhys frowned down at her. "Don't get too excited. Not yet."

"Why not? No more ooze. No more glowing orb. We ended the curse. And you know what that calls for?"

"What's that?"

"A celebration."

"*No*, rest," he said.

Emery pulled away from him and hurried down the stone steps. "Just try to stop me, old man!"

After the weird, crazy, chaotic last forty-eight hours she'd endured, it was time to let loose. Emery deserved this, goddammit.

And Rhys wasn't gonna take this away from her.

CHAPTER 21

EMERY

THANKFULLY, ONCE THEY RETURNED TO HOUSE ROMAN, AND Kat and Dane and the others learned of what happened, the party train quickly left the station, and there was nothing Rhys could do to turn it around.

Dane quickly provided Emery with a margarita, and Emery quickly downed it.

Soon the house's parlor was full of people and revelry. Emery didn't even bother to ask if they were all vampires and if she needed to be worried. She figured if she had Rhys as her protector, no one would harm a hair on her head.

And he was awfully protective of her.

He didn't let her out of his sight, and when someone turned up the music and Emery joined dancers on the makeshift dance floor, she felt Rhys's eyes on her the entire time.

The music pumped through the room and pulsed through Emery's body. Though her drinks had been small, and she didn't feel drunk, she was flying high on euphoria.

Was that the curse? And why the hell could she, of all people, end it?

Did it even matter?

She was a little loopy with the victory and a little high on the fantasy she was currently living.

"This is amazing! Everything is amazing!" she shouted as she downed the rest of her margarita and deposited the glass on an end table. Dane laughed beside her, his body moving with the music in a way that could only be described as delicious.

"You've done well tonight, poppet," Dane said as he danced closer. "You saved the day."

Emery lifted her arms in the air as the bass beat trembled through the floor. "I did, didn't I? Who would have thought an executive assistant could save the day?!"

"*Assistant*—has Rhys not told you yet?"

"Told me what?"

Dane shook his head. "Never mind. Dance, poppet. Dance like your life depends on it."

So she did, and Dane laughed and danced along with her.

The crowd pulsed closer, and Emery caught sight of vampire eyes glowing everywhere, fangs flashing in the overhead light.

She was at a vampire party.

A VAMPIRE PARTY.

How was this her life? How could she ever go back to her normal life after something like this? She didn't want to. She wanted to hang out here every night for the rest of her life. If Rhys wanted her to, anyway. Maybe he didn't.

The music switched to a pop song, and Emery's body swayed with it. She closed her eyes to the punchy beats, and when Dane reached out for her, she let him. His hands slid down her body, lighting a fire in their wake.

Emery was suddenly ravenous.

She opened her eyes and sucked in a breath.

It wasn't Dane moving sensuously with her.

It was Rhys.

His eyes glowed with blue fire, his pupils throbbing.

The center of Emery clenched up, tingling. Rhys's nostrils flared as his hands sunk to her ass, coaxing her into him. She could feel the hardness of his cock through his pants, and that made Emery even hotter.

Everything seemed to slow. The breath in her lungs and the beat of the music and the press of the crowd.

Emery didn't want this to end.

Rhys's fangs elongated, and Emery wiggled her body against his, pushing out her chest, arching her back.

Was she enticing him?

Fuck yeah she was.

Suddenly, his arms were around her, and her feet left the floor, and the world blurred as he carried her with vampire speed from the parlor to a quiet, dark bedroom.

The music still pulsed in the distance, but now Emery could hear the rapid pant of her breath over it.

Rhys's hand came to her jaw, his thumb on her bottom lip, coaxing her mouth open. She sucked his thumb into her mouth and felt the answering pulse of his cock at her waist.

"I shouldn't have brought you here," he said, his eyes still blue molten in the dark.

"Why?"

He rubbed his wet thumb over her bottom lip, and a growl rumbled in his chest. "Because we don't know what the curse has done to you. Or to me. And right now, I want to sink my teeth into you so badly, I'm afraid I won't be able to stop myself."

Emery's heart beat faster in her chest, and nervous butterflies filled her stomach. "So don't stop yourself."

His grip on her tightened, fingers pressing into her jaw. He forced her head back, baring her neck. His cock dug into her, and new wetness turned her slick.

She wasn't sure what she wanted more, his cock inside of her or his teeth in her flesh.

He bent over her, his nose against her skin. He inhaled her scent, and Emery shivered.

"You smell so fucking sweet," he said, his voice heavy and hoarse.

Rhys swung her around and pressed her against the edge of a desk. She had no idea where they were, or whose desk this was, and she didn't care.

She had a flash of Rhys's earlier fantasy, of bending her over the desk. Was he playing out that fantasy? She wouldn't mind it one bit.

"I have to ask you something," she said, breathy.

"Go on." He inhaled again.

"How often do you do this with other women? Is this a regular thing?"

What she didn't say was, *am I special*?

She didn't want to need it, but she did. She didn't want to just be another conquest, just any girl.

She recognized that he'd been around a very long time, and that if he wanted to take a girl home with him, likely there was no one to stop him.

But she wanted to be special.

His glowing eyes met hers, and his fangs flashed in the dim moonlight. "From the moment I first laid eyes on you," he said, "I've been unable to think of anything else. I've danced with madness. I've gone to the edge just to feel the thrill of it. But no woman has ever made me feel so delirious with *need*."

Oh *fuck*.

His hands came to her waist, his fingers slipping beneath the thin material of her t-shirt. His touch caused a shock wave through her body.

"To answer your question, there is nothing regular about this, Emery Blake. Nothing ordinary about you."

Tears burned at her eyes, and her cheeks flushed beneath his words.

That was the single most heartfelt thing anyone had ever said to her.

She brought her hands to his face and pulled him into her and kissed him. His tongue flicked out to meet hers, and the caress of it mixed with the sharp point of his fangs sent a jolt of exhilaration through her.

Their kiss deepened, and they bumped against the table as Emery tried wrestling out of her clothes. Emery couldn't get undressed fast enough, so Rhys helped her to it by ripping off her shirt, then her bra.

It all happened so fast that when she finally stood naked before him, she hadn't been given the chance to worry about what he'd think of her not-exactly-skinny mortal body.

But his hungry gaze told her enough.

He liked what he saw, and the answering thrill buzzing down Emery's spine made every hollow of her body light with fire.

"You are amazing," he said.

She giggled, because she'd lost her damn mind apparently, and said, "Don't make me be the only one standing here naked." She snapped her fingers at him. "Don't make me wait."

His mouth tilted into an amused grin. He took up the hem of his shirt and lifted it over his head.

"Oh...oh God," Emery said.

Every muscle in his stomach was perfectly outlined by deep, shadowed ridges. His long torso tapered to a delicious V, a trail of dark hair disappearing beneath the waist of his pants.

Emery couldn't breathe.

Fuck he was hot.

How the hell was she so damn lucky?

He slowly unbuttoned his jeans and took them off. His boxer briefs were black, but Emery could see the long, hard outline of his cock.

Her breath fluttered in her throat when his hands went to his boxers and tugged them down.

"Holy hell," she whispered when his cock bobbed heavy and free.

He took his shaft in hand and slowly stroked it, and Emery's inner walls clenched up tight, her clit throbbing at just the sight of him.

She wasn't prepared for this.

She wasn't prepared for his Adonis form with the supernatural glow of his eyes and the sharp point of his fangs and the way he looked at her like he wanted to devour her, like he *could*.

From here on out, there would be Before-Rhys Emery and After-Rhys Emery. There would be a clear delineation on the calendar because he would irrevocably change her.

"Are you sure you want to do this?" he asked.

Emery might have imagined it, but she thought she heard a dark challenge in his voice. She almost laughed at the absurdity of it. Was she sure? She was never sure about anything in her life. Was she going to put her clothes back on and turn away from him? Fuck no.

"It would take a nuclear apocalypse to drag me away from this bedroom, from you," she said, because that was the truth.

Rhys was a blur when he rushed to her. Suddenly, she was in his arms again, and his cock was digging at her belly. His fangs were sharp in the moonlight.

"I'll try to be gentle," he said.

She smiled up at him. "I promise I don't break easily."

A rumble sounded in his chest. He tipped her chin back, opened his mouth, and bit her.

The adrenaline rush surged through Emery as the sharp pain burned down her throat. She cried out and bucked instinctively. She was the doe, and Rhys was the predator, and everything encoded in her DNA said to run.

But Rhys tightened his hold on her, caging her against the table, and soon the pain was turning into a buzzing pleasure deep in her bones.

Warmth flooded her veins as a new slickness coated her folds. Rhys's cock slipped into the channel between her legs, and when he rocked his hips, dragging the head of his shaft over her clit, she moaned loudly.

Rhys tightened his grip, sucked harder at her throat.

Oh god. This was...this was...

No words.

She had no words for what this was.

Emery went boneless, a little delirious and lightheaded. Rhys pulled back.

"I better stop before I take too much," he said.

Emery looked at him through heavy lids. His tongue ran over his lips, lapping up her blood, and the imagery made her pussy clench up, thinking of what he might do with that clever tongue of his.

"I feel drunk," she said.

"It's from blood loss," he answered and sucked a drop of blood from his thumb. "Fuck, you taste sweet too."

Emery giggled and listed to the side.

Rhys picked her up easily, his cock finding her warm center.

"You better fill me back up," she said.

Rhys laughed as he carried her to the bed. "Is that right?"

"That's right."

He lay her back, her head nestling amongst the silky pillows. He nudged her knees open and sunk down between them. His hot breath fanned over her folds.

"Oh God," she said, breathy.

"What is it?" Rhys sounded alarmed.

"If you go down there, I think I might come in like two seconds."

He clamped his hand over her mound, and Emery writhed. He wasn't even rubbing her, and she was peaking. Fuck. She didn't want to come already. She didn't want this to end so soon!

"Rhys," she moaned. "I—"

He shifted his hand so his thumb was at her opening. He slowly pushed inside of her, and Emery could hear how wet she was.

"Rhys," she said again. "I don't know—" She panted as he drew his thumb out and pressed in again. He flicked his index finger over her clit, and Emery nearly floated off into the moonlight; it felt so fucking good.

"I don't want to come without you," she managed to get out.

"Don't worry. You're going to come for me at least twice."

"I don't know if I can do that."

Come twice in one night? That had never happened to her.

"You will," Rhys said firmly, as if there was no question.

Then he sunk to her wet folds and lapped up her wetness, and Emery came. She cried out as his tongue flattened over her clit, and then her legs tightened around him as the wave of pleasure made her want to curl up like a leaf.

Rhys wrapped his hands around her thighs and forced her back open as he plunged his tongue inside of her.

White stars burst behind Emery's eyelids as wave after wave crashed through her, and her body tensed and jolted and rode the wave, Rhys's mouth on her the whole time, as if he wanted to taste every note of her orgasm.

When the pleasure had finally ebbed out, Emery sunk into the mattress, sapped.

Rhys sat up, Emery's pleasure still wet on his lips.

Emery blinked through the bliss. "Oh my god. That was...you are..."

Hands at her waist, Rhys dragged her back up and plunged inside of her.

This man kept his promises.

CHAPTER 22

RHYS

Rhys was fucking soaring on the sweet taste of her pussy and her blood.

And when he was firmly seated inside of her and her inner walls pulsed around him, he worried he might just permanently descend into madness.

She was so fucking good.

All of her.

Every part of her.

She drove away his chill and filled his veins with honey.

For the first time in a very long time, Rhys was happy.

There was no curse. No impending doom.

And now, he had Emery.

And he was never going to let her go.

As she moaned, her mouth at his ear, and her pussy throbbing around him, Rhys wondered how he'd gotten so lucky. He'd never believed in luck, but he might be changing his mind.

"I'm going to come again," she said. "Oh fuck. Oh fuck Rhys."

She wrapped her arms around his neck and used him as leverage to grind against his cock, and he braced her, his hands on her hips, as he drove harder and harder into her.

When Emery's slick wet pussy pulsed around him, Rhys lost it. He came deep inside of her. Emery quivered as she reached the edge again and fell with him into the pool of pleasure.

Both of them collapsed on the bed, limbs tangled with one another.

Rhys blinked up at the ceiling.

"That was..." Emery inhaled deeply. "Wow. It was...wow."

Rhys looked over at her and caught sight of the raw bite at her neck. "Stay there," he said and raced to the bathroom and back out again. He returned with a warm, wet cloth and nudged her chin to get a better look at the bite.

"Does it hurt?" he asked.

She smiled sleepily up at him. "Not at all."

Gently, he cleaned the blood away and assessed the bite. He'd been so caught up, he couldn't remember how careful he'd been. But the bite looked like it was already healing. No need to bandage it then.

Mortals usually took several days to heal, but...someone like Emery...she might only need a day if that.

When should he tell her?

He needed to wait. He needed to speak with Kat first.

Rhys blurred away again to toss the cloth in the tub, then quickly returned to Emery. Her eyes were closed, and her breathing was settling into the even breath of sleep.

With the moon already descending, Rhys closed the window shutters, then drew the heavy drapes. Once the room was secure, he crawled into bed beside Emery and pulled her into the crook of his arm.

"Emery," he whispered.

"Mmmm?"

"If you wake before I do, be sure to leave the windows covered."

"Mmm. Why?"

"Otherwise, I'll burst into ash."

She moaned into him and snuggled closer. "Not on my watch," she said, voice muzzy and distant.

"Goodnight," Rhys said to her.

But she was already sleeping.

CHAPTER 23

EMERY

Emery woke chilled and with a stomachache that was so bad, it almost brought her to tears.

She climbed out of bed, disoriented. It was so dark and she was...where was she again?

Right, in Rhys's room.

She kept waking up in strange places.

Her stomach clenched again, and Emery instinctively clamped her hand over her mouth as the urge to vomit overwhelmed her.

Bathroom. Where was the bathroom?

She bumped into the desk, them bumped into an end table. She didn't know where the light switch was, and there was that fuzzy memory of Rhys warning her not to open the blinds.

It was impossible to tell what time it was.

When her feet found a cool, tiled floor, she hurried inside and pawed at the walls.

Where was the damn light switch?

Her stomach somersaulted, and Emery retched.

Shit, no time for lights.

She groped around until her hands found the glass surround of the shower, and she doubled over and vomited.

Even in the darkness, Emery's head swam. She fell to her knees and braced herself on the edge of the shower just to keep herself from falling over.

When her stomach was empty, she sucked in a breath as tears streamed down her face.

She hadn't drunk that much, had she?

She'd been buzzy and tipsy, but not drunk.

Every bone in her body ached, and her chest was so tight, it felt like there was a rubber band around her.

Maybe vampires drank extra-extra strong margaritas, and she just hadn't noticed?

The overhead light flicked on, and Emery blinked against it, the sudden brightness stinging her eyes.

"Emery?" Rhys said, and then, "Emery!"

"I'm okay," she said, her throat raw. "I'm so sorry about this. I'll clean it up—"

"Kat!" he shouted.

Emery blinked up at him. "I said I'm okay. You don't have to call—"

"Kat!" he roared.

Why was he freaking out? He didn't need to broadcast to the entire house that she, Emery Blake, mortal nerd, couldn't hold her liquor.

And then she looked at the shower floor.

The tile was black.

Oily and slick.

Black just like the curse.

CHAPTER 24

EMERY

Apparently, when Rhys shouted for help, the entire house came running.

He'd been kind enough to wrap Emery in a bed sheet before anyone walked through the door, so now Emery sat on the edge of the bed, wearing what amounted to a toga.

The room had quickly filled with vampires, but Rhys shooed most of them out, leaving only Kat and Dane.

Kat stood in front of Emery, her hands held out before her like she was testing the warmth of a fire.

"Tell me what it is," Rhys said, his arms crossed over his chest. He'd slipped on a pair of jeans, but Emery had noted he'd forgone the boxer briefs, so he was currently commando and even though she'd just ralphed black ooze and was maybe about to spontaneously combust from said black ooze, she couldn't help but think about Rhys only having one layer of material between Emery and his junk.

Her junk.

Maybe?

She wasn't sure what this was between them, but damn if she didn't want it to end.

Good thing he couldn't read *her* mind.

"Kat," Rhys said, his voice edging on a growl.

"It's not good," Kat said. "So let's just get that out there."

"But how *bad*?" Dane asked. His stance was a near echo of Rhys's. He stood with feet planted, arms crossed over his chest. His dark hair was rumpled on one side like he'd just rolled out of bed.

"Well…" Kat raked her teeth over her bottom lip as she regarded Emery and opened her thoughts to her.

The prognosis isn't good, Kat thought. *And I'm not sure how Rhys will react once I tell him. You've been warned. Don't be afraid though. Dane and I are here, okay?*

Emery gave a barely perceptible nod.

Kat set her hands on her hips and turned to Rhys and Dane. "It seems as though she didn't end the curse, she just transferred it. It's now growing inside of her."

Rhys growled and turned away, his hand in his hair.

The air was charged, but oddly quiet and calm, like the eye of a storm.

Dane inhaled and uncrossed his arms and loosened up his body like a footballer on the field ready for a charge.

In a blur, Rhys crossed the room, grabbed the bottom of the desk, and hurled it end over end. He roared as it smashed against the wall.

Emery clutched tighter at her toga, instinct telling her to run away.

But no, she'd stand her ground. She was not afraid of Rhys.

Kat and Dane formed a protective circle around her.

You risked her life, and for what? She's not someone to just cast aside. You're too fucking impulsive. You didn't think.

Emery stood up when Rhys's thoughts came to her like ice in a snow storm, sharp and cold.

This is the real curse. Find something you can love and then fucking destroy it.

Mad son of a mad king.

Emery slipped between Dane and Kat.

"I wouldn't—" Kat said.

"Poppet," Dane warned.

"It's okay," Emery said and stepped forward as Rhys raged on.

He threw a lamp, and the glass shattered. He picked up a chair by the legs and cocked it behind one shoulder ready to lob it across the room.

Emery stepped in his line of sight.

He froze, his molten eyes glowing in the dimness.

"Don't," she said.

Pain was etched on his face.

"Please," she said. "Don't."

A deep frown shadowed his eyes.

"I don't like seeing you like this," she said and edged around the fact that she could hear him blaming himself. It wasn't his fault. It wasn't like he created that curse or hid that necklace in an abandoned tunnel. And it wasn't like he told her to walk into said tunnel and touch the damn magical necklace.

"It's not your fault," she said.

Rhys heaved a breath and set the chair down. His mental shield had come up again, and Emery couldn't hear whatever his answering thought was.

"I am not without blame," he said.

"We've faced worse," Dane said. "I'm sure we can figure out a solution to this too."

"Worse?" Rhys snorted. "Don't be a fool, Dane."

Kat came over and took Emery's hand in hers. Kat's skin was cold to the touch. "It might be a long shot, but if you moved the curse to yourself, we might be able to move the curse to something else. Another object." She tossed a look back at Rhys. "Our problem in Last Vale was always that the curse was rooted to that spot. If Emery's successfully moved it, we might—"

"No," Rhys bit out. "I'm tired of temporary solutions."

He paced in a circle in the center of the room, his head bowed as he thought. Emery could tell that here, he was in charge, and that Dane and Kat were waiting for him to make a decision.

"So what do you want to do?" Kat asked.

Emery clutched tighter at the sheet wrapped around her body. She was starting to shiver and sweat at the same time.

Her head was suddenly swimmy and achy.

"I'm going to Ciri," Rhys finally said.

"Umm...bad idea," Dane said.

"Who's Ciri?" Emery asked.

"I would caution you to rethink this course of action and —" Rhys cut Kat off with a sharp look.

"Take care of Emery until I get back," he said.

"Who's Ciri?" Emery asked again as she widened her eyes as if that would somehow stop her head from spinning.

Without another look at her, Rhys exited the room. Emery leapt to her feet to run after him, but her vision teetered, and she lost her balance.

Dane caught her as Kat hooked her beneath the arm.

"Slow down, poppet," Dane said.

"Where is he going?" Emery asked as they helped her back to the bed.

How was it possible that twelve hours ago, she'd been

high on euphoria, and now, she felt like she'd come down with the worst case of the flu?

Oh right, probably that black oozy curse running through her veins.

She was so tired and achy, and now, her head was pounding, and when her eyes were open, her vision burned and flashed like she'd spent too much time looking at the sun.

"Come on, poppet." Dane lifted her onto the bed.

Her arms and legs felt full of lead, and so she didn't fight Dane at all.

"Sleep," Kat said. "I promise you, we'll figure this out."

Sleep did sound good. Maybe if she just rested, maybe it'd go away on its own.

Emery gave in to the rising tide of exhaustion and swam into its darkness.

CHAPTER 25

RHYS

Rhys drove north along M-12 where the road wound along the coast. The ocean crashed against the shoreline.

What the fuck had he been thinking, taking Emery to Last Vale?

They were running blind, and he'd allowed himself to be swayed by the possibilities before he thought through the consequences.

What if they couldn't fix Emery?

What if he'd ruined her?

And he still hadn't told her what she was.

When she found out he'd kept it from her—

The leather of the steering wheel groaned as Rhys adjusted his death grip.

His rational side told him Emery was just another girl. One girl out of the thousands he'd come into contact with over his lifetime.

But she wasn't just any girl, was she?

Emery was funny and kind, and she caught him off guard with nothing more than her clever wit.

When you got to be as old as he was, it was extremely hard to be surprised. And Emery surprised him at every turn.

Rhys drove up the driveway that led to the Queen of the Oracle's house and stopped at the closed gate. He rolled down the window and caught the tangy taste of salty sea air. He reached out and pressed the call button on the security system.

"We're not taking visitors," a voice said from the other side.

"It's Rhys Roman," he answered.

"Again, we're not taking visitors. Come back another day."

The speaker crackled as the call was ended.

Rhys pushed the button again.

"Sir, the Queen is—"

"I don't care what she's doing. Tell her she'll see me now or I'll burn this fucking place to the ground."

The speaker was silent for several minutes. The leather steering wheel groaned again, and Rhys gritted his teeth.

"The Queen has ten minutes for you," the speaker said. "Ten minutes and no more."

The gate clanked open, and Rhys drove inside.

The driveway ascended up the hillside through a strip of woods that let out to a massive beach house that overlooked the ocean.

The house was a sprawling estate with numerous windows, so almost every vantage point had a view of the ocean. Now the windows glowed golden in the growing dusk.

Rhys parked in the wrap-around driveway and got out.

The front door was pulled open by a young woman in a gauzy white dress.

Rhys didn't know many of the Oracles by name, but he knew this one.

In his mind, he'd named her Brownie because she reminded him of the fae brownies that used to visit Last Vale from time to time. They were always short and slight with big, wide eyes.

This girl had blunt bangs that hung in front of her eyes when she blinked up at him. "Right this way," she said in that eerie Oracle voice.

She led him through the house's living room and out through sliding doors to the back deck. The deck ran the length of the sprawling house, with several sitting areas dotted around it.

Rhys caught sight of Ciri on the left. She sat stretched out on a chaise lounge beside a raised stone fire pit. A fire blazed in the pit, embers trailing up into the darkness.

Ciri wore a silk robe and a vintage swimsuit—the kind women had been made to wear in the early 1900s. Her black hair hung in perfect waves around her face.

Horn-rimmed sunglasses hid her eyes despite the darkening sky.

Rhys had only seen the queen's eyes once, and it wasn't a pleasant sight. She had no irises, no pupils.

It was a sight that could shake any man, even a vampiric one.

"What a pleasure to see you again, Mr. Roman," the queen purred and raised her glass of red wine to her mouth.

Rhys joined her at the fire pit and sat in a chair across from her.

"What brings you here tonight," the queen asked.

"I suspect you already know."

"Mmmm." The queen took another sip of wine. "The air feels different already, doesn't it? A little lighter."

"You gave me the solution and told me none of the consequences."

"Do you mean the girl? Why do you care?"

Everyone kept asking him that, and he still had no good answer.

Rhys sat forward, elbows on his knees, and lowered his voice, feeling the rumble of anger deep in his chest. "Tell me how to fix it."

The queen clucked her tongue. "You wanted to end the curse. You ended it."

"Not at the expense of an innocent life."

"But is she innocent?" Ciri wrinkled her nose. "Her lineage is no ally of yours. You owe her nothing."

"She shouldn't have to die for this. The curse is mine to bear. Not hers."

"Awww." The queen pushed out her bottom lip in a mocking pout. "She's just one girl. Disposable really."

Rhys clenched his teeth. "Emery is *not* disposable."

"No?" Ciri sat forward, her fingers curled around the globe of her wine glass. "If I'd told you this would be the outcome, that in order to end the curse, you'd have to sacrifice one girl, would you have gone through with it?"

"Of course not."

She raised a brow. "Really? I think you're lying to yourself."

Rhys opened his mouth to argue and quickly clamped it shut again. Because the truth was...if he'd known all along that Emery wouldn't survive, he would never have allowed himself to get close to her.

The man he was before Emery, just a few days ago, was a man who very much would have thought one life in exchange for ending the curse was a sacrifice worth pursuing.

"How do I fix her?" he asked again, his voice low and nearly trembling.

The queen laughed, the trill of it ringing out over the crash of ocean waves "You can't."

His stomach twisted with regret and fear. "There has to be a way."

"Oh sure, of course there's a way. The curse is in her blood. Drain her of blood and the curse will die."

"She won't survive that!" Rhys said with a growl.

Ciri sat back against her lounge chair, crossed her legs, and clasped her hands over her middle. "Your time is up, Mr. Roman. Run along before I burn *you* to the ground."

With a growl, Rhys pushed off the chair and left.

CHAPTER 26

EMERY

Everything ached.

Emery felt like a child again, curled in her bed with the flu while her mother took care of her through the pain and discomfort and delirium.

Except this time, it wasn't her mother, it was a witch.

"This should help for the fever," Kat said and helped Emery into a sitting position. Then she handed over a mug of something hot.

The steam might have been warm on Emery's face, but she couldn't tell. She was shivering and burning up at the same time.

"What is it?"

"An elixir my grams used to make for me," Kat explained. "No magic. Just herbs."

It smelled like lemons and honey and something earthy.

Emery took a tentative sip. In every fantasy movie she'd ever watched, when a witch offered an elixir, it usually tasted like shit. But this was surprisingly good, and as the liquid warmed her belly, some of the constant churning in her gut settled too.

"That is actually helping," Emery said and lay her head back against the bed. "Thank you."

"You're welcome."

She was still in Rhys's room, sweating in his pretty sheets. How long had he been gone? She barely remembered going to sleep earlier before he'd left, and she had no idea how long she'd been out.

The fever was making everything feel surreal. She could have crossed over to Alius and have no clue.

"How long have you been with Rhys?" Emery asked as she clutched at the mug of tea. The heat through the earthenware was helping with the fever chill too.

Kat pulled one of the wingback chairs over to the bedside and sat. "He saved me from a witch trial in England in the 1600s. He was of the nobility and had me pardoned." She waggled her hand in front of her face. "Of course, he may or may not have used his ability to enthrall to make that happen. Vampire mind control is a power I've always coveted."

"How does that work anyway?"

"They just look at you, pull you in, and—" she snapped her fingers, "—that's it. Most people don't have a hope of fighting against it, though it's an ability that takes years to master. And Rhys has definitely had the time to perfect it."

That made Emery wonder...

"Has he used it on me?"

She might have already been flush with fever, but the thought of him using that power to have sex with her made a fresh bloom of scarlet appear across her face.

Kat patted Emery on the arm. "Don't worry. I know Rhys

well, and he doesn't use enthralling very often, and certainly not on a pretty lady."

Emery smiled. "Thanks Kat. For...well...everything. But especially this tea."

Emery sipped from the mug. It really did feel like the fever was coming down. She wasn't shivering as much as she had been.

Rhys returned home not long after Emery finished her tea. He immediately came to her bedside, concern sharpening the lines of his face.

"How are you feeling?" he asked.

"Better." Emery was nestled into the pillows, the tea doing its job. She really did feel loads better. Maybe everything would turn out all right. Maybe Emery and the necklace had somehow absorbed the curse, and her body was now purging it like an actual virus.

"I'm glad to hear it," Rhys said, but the dark circles beneath his eyes said he wasn't glad about anything right now. Something was bothering him.

"Where did you go?" Emery asked.

"To see a friend," he answered.

He and Kat shared a look.

Emery pulled herself up against the headboard. "What is going on?"

Rhys completely ignored her and stood up. "Kat, can I speak with you for a moment?"

"Rhys," Emery said, surprising herself with the sharp tone of her voice. He might be a several-hundred-year-old vampire, but she didn't like him constantly pushing her out.

"I'll be back," he promised her. "I just need to speak with Kat."

Kat got up and followed him out the door.

Emery grumbled and collapsed against the headboard. She wasn't a child! She didn't need to be coddled.

What was he so afraid of her finding out?

Just the thought of all the possibilities had her stomach aching again.

Was it the curse? The mind reading? Rhys had said vampires could shield their minds because there had been others like Emery.

Did he know something she didn't? Well, the answer to that was obvious. Yes, he definitely knew a lot more than she did.

Well maybe she'd just find out on her own if he insisted on keeping things from her.

She threw back the blankets. The sheets were still damp with her sweat, but her skin was no longer hot to the touch. Whatever that elixir was, Kat's gram's magic had done the trick.

Emery kept her steps light as she went to the door and poked her head into the hallway. Was it physically possible to spy on a vampire?

Probably Rhys could already hear her heartbeat, and probably he could already hear her footsteps as she crossed the hallway.

But it was certainly worth a shot, right?

Please don't catch me eavesdropping, she said over and over in her head, and as she thought it, turning it into a mantra, her hands tingled and her heart beat a little harder, and a rush of that euphoria ran through her.

Okay what was that?

Voices filtered into her head.

Whoa.

It was like listening to someone's thoughts but...at a distance. She had to strain to hear.

She went absolutely still and held her breath.

"What did the old hag have to say?" Kat asked.

Rhys was silent for a moment and then, "She didn't say it outright, but she certainly alluded to it. Emery appears to be exactly what we suspected."

Emery reeled back. What the hell? What did they suspect she was?

"Well, the mark told us as much."

Emery pulled the collar of her shirt aside to look at the tattoo on her skin. This mark? She knew it meant more than they were telling her. But what, exactly?

"It still doesn't explain how she's connected to the curse," Rhys said.

"Right. Okay. Let me think for a second."

Though Emery couldn't see into the room, she pictured Kat pacing, her arms crossed over her middle. It was weird —the sounds coming to her ears were only the words spoken aloud. She couldn't hear any other ambient noise. Not footsteps, or floorboards creaking.

"What do we know about the Ravenwoods?" Kat said.

The tingling intensified up and down Emery's arms as goosebumps erupted on her skin.

The Ravenwoods. The Wood family.

"They're vindictive," Rhys said.

"Yeah. And they always loved a good twist."

There was another beat of silence, and Emery bit at her bottom lip fighting against the urge to walk closer to the closed door down the hall.

If she so much as hit a creaky floorboard, she'd be caught.

Did they already know she was there? What were they doing? Why weren't they speaking?

And then—

"Fucking hell." Rhys growled. "They didn't use Raven-wood blood to kindle the curse. They used demon blood."

Emery clamped her hand over her mouth as a startled gasp threatened to escape her.

What the fuck?

This...*she*...were they...

They weren't suggesting she was a *demon*?

"That makes a lot of sense, actually," Kat said. "Think about it. The curse affects your mental stability and what are demons known for?"

"Fucking with your mind."

"Mmmhmm," Kat said. "The Ravenwoods must have stripped Emery's family of their demon mark centuries ago to bind their magic so they wouldn't be a threat. And they hid the mark away in that tunnel—"

Emery looked down at the mark again and traced her finger over one of the twining lines.

This couldn't possibly be true.

Could it?

But Emery could feel something fracturing inside of her, like an illusion cracking, falling away.

She'd never felt like she fit. Not in her normal life. Not in her so-called family.

She'd always felt like an outlier, and she'd blamed it on the whole mind-reading ability, but...maybe there was more.

Way more.

And if she accepted that she was different, then that meant Rhys and Kat and probably Dane had been keeping it from her this entire time.

They knew exactly who and what she was, and they hadn't told her.

And when Rhys fucked her—

Goddammit.

Fucking hell.

He'd lied to her.

Tears burned in her eyes. She was out of her depth here.

"We've been looking for the wrong key this entire time," Kat went on. "And undoing the curse bears no risk for the Ravenwoods because—."

"Because it's Emery's life that is on the line, not theirs."

"Did Ciri say anything about how to undo it?"

Emery braced herself as the tears blurred her vision.

"The curse is in her blood now," Rhys answered. "Drain her of all blood, and you kill the curse."

Emery went cold and woozy. She stepped back, swayed, and caught herself on the wall.

Oh god.

Oh god.

She had to die to end the curse?

And what did Rhys want more than anything?

To end the curse that had been plaguing him and Last Vale for centuries.

And who was she to him? Some random girl who meant nothing to him.

Rhys Roman was a billionaire vampire king.

If he wanted her dead, he'd find a way.

She needed to go.

Right now.

She needed to hide.

How the fuck did you hide from a vampire?

Well, she was going to do her damnedest to find a way.

Emery turned around and ran.

CHAPTER 27

EMERY

EMERY HAD NO CAR AND NO PURSE, AND SHE WAS PRETTY SURE her phone was still at House Roman.

She literally had nothing.

Not even shoes.

She'd watched a lot of movies in her lifetime, and whenever she watched a drama or a suspense movie where a woman found herself running from the bad guy, half clothed, barefoot, she liked to think: *that is the worst! But my life is so boring, that will never be me. And thank god for that.*

And now here she was, stumbling down a busy street in the middle of Second Quarter, running from someone who wanted to kill her, and all she could think was: what am I stepping on?

She spotted a woman scrolling through her phone on the corner of Eight and Baramont.

Emery hurried over to her.

The woman had a kind face and big brown eyes. Her dark hair was in locs with emerald green at the tips.

"Excuse me!" Emery said.

The second the woman set eyes on Emery, a frown deepened the fine lines around her eyes. "Are you okay?" the woman asked.

Emery could only imagine what she looked like.

"Could I borrow your phone? Just for a second?"

The woman's frown turned suspicious.

Emery had to thank the stars she was at least clothed in a t-shirt and leggings!

"What for?" the woman asked.

"I'm—" Emery was about to say *running from a vampire*, but that probably wouldn't go over well. She hated lying, but right now, her life literally depended on it. "I'm running from my boyfriend." Tears burned in her eyes. "I just need to call my friend to come get me. Please. I left my phone at his house."

The woman looked at Emery with new eyes now, and concern turned her mouth down at the corners. "Of course. Here." She handed the phone over.

"Thank you so much."

Emery quickly punched in Morgan's phone number and brought it to her ear. The phone rang and rang. *Come on, Morgan!*

She got the voicemail after only three rings.

"Shit." She ended the call.

"Is there someone else you can try?" the woman said.

Emery had very few phone numbers memorized, and she sure as hell wasn't calling Tanner. Beth it was. Thankfully her cousin picked up on the second ring, and oddly enough, she sounded worried.

"Em, where have you been? We've been looking everywhere for you!"

That was super not like her cousin. "Can you come pick me up?"

"For sure. Where are you?"

Emery didn't want to stay on Eighth Street. It was too close to House Roman.

"Meet me on the corner of Hill Street and Washington."

"Okay. I'm leaving now."

"Thanks Beth."

"No worries, cuz. I'll see you in a bit."

Emery ended the call. She was at least a mile away from the intersection so she needed to get moving. She handed the phone back to the woman. "Thank you so much. You have no idea."

"Of course, sweetie. Good luck. Don't take no shit, all right?"

Emery managed a smile. "I won't."

She hurried off down the street, barefoot and determined more than ever.

WHEN BETH PULLED up in her car, Emery nearly wept with relief. Her feet were aching, and her head was pounding, and she was pretty sure the fever had returned. She hadn't barfed black slime yet, but the longer she stood in the wet heat of the night, the more her stomach churned.

Kat's elixir was starting to wear off. What the hell was Emery going to do now?

Who was going to help her figure this shit out? It wasn't like she could go to her doctor and ask for an antibiotic.

One step at a time.

The first thing she needed to do was get home, get

changed, put on some damn shoes and then figure out the next step.

Beth put the car in park, but left the engine idling. She climbed out and looked Emery up and down. "What the hell happened to you?"

"Long story." Emery was aware that she looked like she'd been kidnapped and stuffed in a dungeon, but there was no time for an explanation, and anyway, Beth wasn't the person Emery wanted to confide in. "Can you just take me home?"

"Totally." Beth got behind the wheel again, and Emery slid into the passenger seat.

Her head was swimming again, the world spinning.

Once she was buckled and Beth had the car in drive and pulled away from the curb, Emery slouched in her seat and covered her eyes with her hand. It might have been well after sunset, but her eyes were burning as if it were high noon.

She'd just rest her eyes for a second as Beth took them home, but as soon as the car was moving, Emery was out.

CHAPTER 28

RHYS

"So what do you want to do?" Kat asked.

Rhys turned away from her and paced to the window that overlooked the bay. It was always night in his world, always darkness and shadows. He was several hundred years old, and in all that time, he'd rarely pined for the sun. As a prince, he'd spent most of his time in seedy taverns anyway, getting drunk, filling the monotony with prostitutes and gambling.

He was the son of a mad king—no one had expected much of him. In fact, Rhys had lived most of his days like it was his last in court. There had always been whispers of deposing his father. Sometimes Rhys had pined for *that*.

He'd never wanted to be a leader. In fact, the responsibility chaffed. A little part of him thought that when he started House Roman, he was starting it only to fail at it. That it was somehow his destiny as it had been his father's.

And once the Ravenwoods bore the curse, Rhys thought, *Finally*.

It was inevitable. He'd just never expected it to take so long.

Now here he was centuries later, reaping what he sowed.

Emery might be the key to his survival, but did he deserve to survive?

"If you were in my position," Rhys said to Kat, his back still to her, "what would you do?"

"The life of one to save many? That's a simple decision to make. But...Emery is...well, she's been growing on me. I won't lie. Demon or not," she finished with a laugh. "Never thought I'd say that, but here we are."

Rhys had always admired Kat for her unique ability to be compassionate and ruthless when the situation called for it.

Rhys crossed his arms over his chest. He was staring at the glowing lights of a barge just outside the bay, but he wasn't really seeing it. His mind was far away.

On a girl.

Kat was right—saving Emery over his vampires didn't make sense. Not to someone in his position, the ruler of a house.

But why did the thought of not saving her make his stomach knot and his throat grow tight?

Why did the thought of losing Emery make him want to break things?

Perhaps wanting to save her was the madness itself.

He put his hands on the windowsill, bowed forward, and closed his eyes.

He knew what he wanted to do.

And that even if he somehow survived, his position as leader of House Roman might be in jeopardy.

Ramses would call him weak. And he wouldn't be wrong.

But Rhys would suffer anything if Emery lived. And didn't she deserve the truth?

Sucking in a deep breath, he made his decision and pushed away from the window, jaw set, shoulders back.

"I know that look," Kat said.

Rhys went around her, ignoring her annoyance and worry, and opened the door. "I'll present Emery with the facts, and she can decide on her own. I will not force her into sacrificing herself for me."

"You can't be serious," Kat said. "She's going to freak out when you tell her she's got demon blood in her lineage."

"She accepted vampires and witches easily enough. And I've already alluded to the fact that she has magic in her blood."

"And you conveniently left out what *kind* of magic," Kat pointed out.

"She'll come around."

He turned into the hallway and found Dane, computer in hand. "I got something."

"Not now," Rhys said. He'd been gone from Emery too long, and he'd left her in the dark too long. She deserved to know what he knew. She deserved to know who and what she was, and how that factored into the curse and—

"This is definitely something you'll want to hear," Dane was saying as Rhys pushed through the door to Emery's room.

But as soon as he was over the threshold, he realized something was wrong. The room was silent. There was no sound of Emery's heartbeat, a now familiar *dah-dum, dah-dum* that he was almost sure he could hear in the back of his head at all times like soothing white noise that calmed his rashness and his constant irritation.

"Where is she?" he said to the room.

He hadn't heard her leave. How the fuck did he not hear her leave?

"Motherfucker," Dane said, "if you'll just listen—"

"I said, not now!" Rhys roared.

Dane frowned at him but did not flinch. He continued, ignoring Rhys's explosion. "I finally dug through some of Emery's history, so yes, *now*. There is no better time than *now*."

Rhys inhaled through his nose and tried to calm his roaring heart. "Go on," he said evenly.

"Emery has been living with a cousin, apparently. It's why I couldn't find her current address. She's using a PO Box."

"Okay?" Rhys said, the irritation returning.

"Her cousin's name is Beth Wood."

A shadow of trepidation came over Rhys.

No.

Fuck. No.

Rhys had smelled Ravenwood on Emery when they'd first met, which could be easily explained by living with a Ravenwood witch.

"Well shit," Kat said.

Hands tightening into fists, Rhys's vision went white with rage.

He was losing it. He was already on the downward slide. He wanted to smash things. Break things. Bones and glass and sink his teeth into a lovely pale throat—

"The Ravenwoods always loved a good twist," Kat said.

Fucking hell they did.

If the Ravenwoods thought they were going to take what was his again, they had another thing coming.

He was used to being one of the most powerful in the

city. He was used to getting his way and being able to protect what was his.

And Emery *was* his. He didn't care who or what she was. He didn't care if he had to choose between her or his entire House.

She was his and his to protect. He could feel it beating like a primal need in his gut.

And if those fucking Ravenwood witches so much as scratched Emery, he would burn their fucking coven to the ground.

"Give me the address," he said.

Dane read it back to him.

Kat stepped forward, a hand held up as if cautioning him. "What's your move here? Think this through."

He had. He did.

He knew what he needed to do.

"Get out of my way, Kat."

There was a brief moment where he considered how far he'd go with his witch in order to get to Emery.

But thankfully, Kat didn't make him chose.

She stepped aside. "Fine. But if you're going, I'm going. You'll need a witch at your back. Give me two minutes to change."

She was wearing her usual clothing: a sharp red dress, cut low in the front and the back. It wasn't the outfit you wore to a battle.

"Two minutes and no more," he said. "Go."

She hurried out the door.

"I'll come too," Dane said, tucking the computer beneath his arm. "We should drink first."

Rhys grumbled an agreement, and they darted down the stairs to the back parlor. Dane set the computer aside and grabbed two bags of blood from the fridge.

"Here." He threw Rhys a bag. "Drink up."

Rhys tore off the cap and choked down one bag. The blood was sludgy going down his throat, and he nearly spat it out. Nothing would ever compare to the fresh stuff, but now it really paled in comparison to the sweet sensation of Emery's blood on the tip of his tongue.

She'd tasted so fucking good.

Of course, now that he knew who and what she was, he realized just how much he'd buried his head in the sand about her.

Of course she'd tasted sweet.

Emery Blake was a demon.

And now she was *his* little demon, and nothing would stop him from saving her.

CHAPTER 29

EMERY

EMERY CAME TO WITH A START.

She barely remembered falling asleep. But hadn't she fallen asleep in the car? Why was she lying down?

There was no way Beth could have carried her into the apartment. Beth was smaller than Emery.

When she opened her eyes, she realized she was in semi-darkness. And not only that, but it was echoey and wet, like a basement.

Or a cave.

What the hell?

Emery sat up, only to realize she couldn't.

Lifting her head as far as she could, she noticed leather straps wrapped around her that were connected to the table beneath her.

"Hey!" Her voice bounced around the room and then back to her. "Is anyone there? Beth? Rhys?"

Maybe Rhys had caught them and kidnapped her? Crap. He was going to murder her!

All Emery wanted was a goddamn promotion!

What the hell had she gotten herself into?

It couldn't end here.

This couldn't be the end of her life!

She still had goals. Things she wanted to accomplish and places she wanted to go.

Tears burned in her eyes, and her chin wobbled.

Fuck. She'd really gotten herself into some shit now.

Please get me out of this.

Please let me live.

She tested the straps around her arms. They were made of old brown leather with weird symbols carved into them. The symbols reminded her of the same symbols on the necklace.

There were more straps across her chest and stomach, another set across her thighs, and two at her ankles.

Even if she managed to break one, there'd still be too many left.

"Hello!" she shouted again.

"You are the noisiest person I've ever met." Beth emerged from the shadows. Her hair was wound up into a messy bun, and she wore a pair of denim overalls and a t-shirt with a faded rainbow on the front.

"Beth." Emery exhaled loudly. "Thank God. Can you get me out of these?"

"Now, why would I go and do that?"

Sleep, *and fear*, still clouded Emery's head. Had she heard Beth right?

She turned to Beth's thoughts and found only silence.

Maybe it was the curse screwing with her ability?

"Beth," Emery said, trying to keep the panic from her voice, "help me get down? There's a vam—I mean, a man...Rhys Roman? You've heard of him, right? He's dangerous, and he's after me, and there's...well...there's something wrong with me. I don't know how I got here and...did he find me somehow? Maybe he enthralled you—"

Beth said, her face blank, "Sometimes you are also the world's biggest idiot."

"What!?"

A second figure emerged from the shadows.

"Aunt Nina?"

"Oh darling." Nina came more into the light. Her hair was braided over one shoulder, several curly tendrils hanging along her heart-shaped face.

"What is going on?" Emery asked, dread welling in her belly.

She couldn't hear her aunt's thoughts either.

She didn't understand why she was strapped to a table, and her aunt and cousin were just casually standing by, but she got the feeling that she'd vastly underestimated the situation, and maybe her cousin and aunt too.

And then she remembered...the conversation with Rhys and Kat in the basement of TS Jenison...the Wood family.

Her family.

Or so she thought.

Beth had always been full of family stories. She loved to brag about her family, about how rich they were, about how her ancestors were mafia-like, and how when someone crossed them, they *took care of them.*

But now that Emery thought about it, Beth had never used the term *mafia.* In her wild imagination, Emery had filled it in with the only likeness she knew at the time.

The truth was so much greater, maybe worse.

Kat had said the Wood family name was just a shortened version of their real name.

"You're the Ravenwood witches," Emery said beneath her breath.

Beth smiled. "Took you fucking long enough."

"Don't be rude, baby," Aunt Nina said. She stepped over to Emery and brushed a lock of hair from Emery's face. "How are you feeling, darling?"

"I'd be feeling better if I wasn't strapped to a table."

Aunt Nina laughed, her voice echoing around the dark space. Did she think this was a joke?

"Rhys said I was a demon and that's insane, right? So if you guys are Ravenwood witches, does that mean I'm a witch too? Did he get it wrong?"

"As if," Beth said with an eye roll. "The vampire was right. You're demon trash."

Emery's heart sunk. But she shouldn't be surprised, right?

For her entire life, she knew she was different. She could hear people's thoughts. Like Rhys, she'd been suffering from a curse for a very long time, one she thought she'd never be rid of.

She'd never thought to question the *why*.

She never thought that having the ability to read minds might mean she was something other than human.

Demon.

She knew it was the truth and yet she still couldn't seem to settle into it, to accept it.

A handful of days ago, she hadn't believed in demons, but now?

And did demons come from Hell? Or that other place —Alius?

Were demons anything like what she'd read about in the history and mythology books?

She didn't feel evil or bad.

The worst thing she did was throw away plastic.

And even then, it had been more to spite Michael than anything else.

There were so many questions, so many things crowding her head. There were so many things left to learn.

Had her mom known? Was her mom—

"Could my mom read minds?" Emery asked.

"She could," Aunt Nina answered. "And that's why we had to *take care of her.*"

CHAPTER 30

RHYS

RHYS PLANTED HIS BOOT ON THE DINGY RED DOOR OF EMERY'S apartment and kicked through it. He had no time for knocking.

The door exploded inward, hinges ripping from the frame, splinters flying like stakes.

"The fuck?" Dane said, his arms up like a shield. "You could have accidentally staked us."

Rhys tested the doorway and found immediate resistance, both witchy and vampiric.

Vampires needed an invitation into inhabited dwellings. It was something pop culture unfortunately got right.

"Kat," Rhys said.

"Yeah, yeah." She waved her hand through the air, and the doorway rippled like the surface of a pond. "It's a pretty good barrier spell, but not good enough." Her vicious red lips twisted into a smirk, and she snapped her fingers. A second later, she was stepping inside.

"Does it look the same as it does from the outside?" Rhys

asked. He'd become adept at spotting illusions over the years, but he wasn't taking any chances.

Kat scanned the space. "Looks as it appears." She wrinkled her nose. "Definitely a Ravenwood house. I feel like I'm drowning in roses."

"Anyone there?" Dane asked.

"I don't think so."

Rhys cursed and paced away. They were on the landing outside the apartment, so there wasn't far to go.

He should have told Emery. He should have been honest with her.

"I can do a locator spell," Kat said.

When Rhys turned back to the apartment door, Kat was slipping into what must have been a bedroom. She came out a few seconds later with a hairbrush and joined them on the landing. She pulled a clump of hair from the bristles and balled it up between the palms of her hands, closing her eyes as she did.

Rhys could immediately smell Emery, the sweetness coupled with the smell of anise.

It'd been so long since he'd encountered a demon, he'd completely forgotten what they smelled like, how they felt. Of course, the demon mark had been stripped from her lineage, her magic bound.

It was no wonder he hadn't realized at first who and what she was.

And if he had?

Demons had never been enemies of the vampires, but they tended to be solitary by nature because of their ability to read and manipulate minds. And the mark was hard to hide.

People, mortal and supernatural, gave demons a wide berth.

And if Rhys had known Emery had demon blood in her lineage upon first meeting, he never would have allowed himself to get close.

It was too late to go back now. He was in. He'd risk everything to save Emery. Even himself.

When Kat opened her eyes, her irises were glowing bright green, but her brow was sunk in a frown.

"What is it?" Rhys asked.

"I found Emery."

"And?"

"And...she's in Last Vale."

CHAPTER 31

EMERY

TAKE CARE OF HER.

Aunt Nina's words echoed through Emery's mind.

"You killed my mother?"

The tears blurred in her eyes, and Emery tightened her hands into fists and fought against the straps.

"How could you!"

She collapsed back against the table. The straps barely gave way.

Aunt Nina barely flinched. "Your mother could read minds," she said, "but she didn't know how or why. She ended up finding out by accident."

Emery blinked, and several tears rolled down her temple.

This was too much.

Too much new information.

Why had her mom never talked about her ability? She knew Emery could read minds too. Emery told her when she was barely five years old. And the whole time she'd thought she was alone, different, damaged.

And her mom had the same ability and kept it from her.

Aunt Nina came to stand beside Emery's shoulder. "Your mother had always been a little too thorough with her research. She uncovered the secrets in some dusty archive somewhere in the city. We would have never realized she'd learned the truth if she hadn't gone looking for others like you."

"What do you mean?"

"When she found out who we were, what she was, she started asking around, asking too many questions. She'd had no idea what she was provoking, so we had to stop her. To protect you and what little of your line is left."

Emery's body went numb as more tears blurred her vision.

"Mom died when the Hawley Bridge collapsed. How—"

"We are Ravenwood witches, dear. Elemental witches. If we need to make a bridge collapse, we can easily make that happen."

Oh Mom.

If only you'd told me!

If only...

And Aunt Nina and Beth...

"You're not actually my family are you?" Emery asked as her throat clogged with the unshed tears.

Aunt Nina shook her head. "I don't even have a brother."

What the actual hell?

"So who is my father?"

Aunt Nina shrugged. "I'm not actually sure. Your mom never said."

Emery's head was spinning now, but she couldn't tell if it

was because she'd been lying down too long, or if she was suffering from some kind of mental breakdown.

Nothing was what she thought it was, and everything was changing, and she was still strapped to a fucking table by a woman who she had believed was her aunt.

"A few hundred years ago, when the Ravenwoods cast the curse that Rhys Roman currently suffers from," Aunt Nina went on, "they used a demon to do it. Someone from your line. I don't know what line you are, and I don't care. Once the curse was born, my ancestors stripped the demon of its mark and bound it. I'm not sure what their plan was from there. The only thing I know is that every ancestor before me has been taught to keep you close, but in the dark, should we need the curse undone. And now here we are."

The tears overwhelmed Emery, her vision immediately going watery.

She was in trouble, and there was no one left to protect her.

She had no one.

And she was a *demon*.

"Shh, shh," Aunt Nina said and brushed the tears from Emery's face. "It's going to be all right, dear."

"I'm strapped to a table!" Emery said through the sobs.

The air grew charged as the assembled women raised their voices.

"Your sacrifice will help the greater good," Nina said.

"What are you talking about?"

"The curse was meant to weaken Mr. Roman. It had unfortunate side effects, of course, and it's been dragging out too long. Our theory is our ancestors didn't factor in the magic of the ley line that ran through Last Vale. It muddied the spell. We were unable to figure out how to correct the curse, considering it was rooted to the land."

Aunt Nina spread out her hands. "With Ciri's help, you've solved that problem for us."

"So I'm no better than a pawn in a sick game."

"No, you're a way for us to fix an error."

"By doing what?"

Aunt Nina folded her hands in front of her as she looked down at Emery. "Kill Rhys Roman and his cursed vampires once and for all and let the witches reign."

CHAPTER 32

RHYS

RHYS DROVE EAST.

His hands were tight on the steering wheel, the leather groaning beneath the strength of his rage and fear.

What if it was too late? What if the fucking Ravenwood witches killed Emery?

What if this was all his fault?

The whole reason Emery was tangled up in this was because of Rhys and his greed. Yes, Last Vale had been his to begin with, but he could have negotiated with the Ravenwoods and let them use the land and its ley line.

The truth was, like his father, Rhys had been moved by greed. Last Vale was his and his alone. He wasn't going to fucking share it.

Now look at what it cost him.

If something happened to Emery, it would be his fault.

The thought of losing her set a pit at the center of him.

The world would pale without Emery in it. There was no

going back. No way for him to be as he was before. Before Emery Blake entered his life.

He would burn those fucking witches.

He would watch them smolder to ash.

When he reached the end of the road where the woods helped shield Last Vale from the rest of the city, Rhys pulled over and put the car in park.

"So you have a plan yet?" Dane asked from the back seat.

There was an idea taking shape in his mind, one that Kat and Dane would very much not like.

They would try to talk him out of it, and they'd be right to dissuade him.

"Kat," he said as he shut the car off and let the engine cool.

"Yes?" Already her voice had taken on an edge of suspicion.

"Do you remember in 1702 when you were facing trial, you linked our lives so that you would live?"

"Yes," she said carefully. "Why?"

"I need you to do that again."

Kat had been hung for suspected witchcraft. The linking spell had allowed her to live using some of Rhys's life to keep her alive. A vampire had a lot of life to give. It came with the immortality.

Dane sat forward, poking his head between the seats. "Are you suggesting Kat link you with Emery?"

"That's exactly what he's suggesting," Kat said with a grumble. "I'm not linking you with a demon. There's no telling what she might do to your mind. She's untrained and host to a curse. Or did you forget about that?"

Rhys turned in the bucket seat. "Kat. I will not ask you again."

"No," she said and shook her head to emphasize the point. "No fucking way."

"Kat."

"Rhys."

Dane sat back. "I'm beginning to think I should exit the vehicle in case this goes sideways."

"You can't control the outcome of this." Kat pressed her back against the passenger side door. "This isn't a hanging and a broken neck. We're talking Ravenwood witches, demon blood. There's too much I can't predict. Too much magic. We don't even know why they took her. What do you think they plan to do with her? Because I can tell you right now, they're not throwing a block party in your honor."

Rhys's blood family had died hundreds of years ago. Kat and Dane were as close as he could get to family now.

Rhys would let her speak her peace before he made her bow to his command.

He might have been the son of a mad king, but curse or madness, it didn't matter—he was fucking leader of his house.

No one would tell him no.

"Kat," he said, his voice even.

Tears welled in her eyes as she raked her teeth over her vicious red lips.

"I don't fucking want to do this," she said.

"I know you don't."

"You're a fucking asshole."

"I know."

She looked away and wiped a tear with the bend of her knuckle. "I don't know if you'll survive."

"We've always known my demise might be imminent. How is this any different?"

Another tear trailed down her face. "Fucking Ravenwood witches. Goddammit. Fine." She pulled the ball of hair from the pocket of her leather leggings. Rhys had caught her saving the hair after the locator spell. Witches could create magic out of nothing, but it was always stronger if they had some other source of energy to tap into. Plants, elements, a ley line...a clump of hair.

"Take off your shirt," Kat said.

Rhys grabbed the t-shirt at the back of his neck and pulled it off in one swift motion. Kat whispered a few words in the old language, the language of witches.

Her eyes flared, and she pressed the ball of hair to Rhys's chest where an old scar still remained from the last time they'd performed this spell.

"*Vita copulare*," she said and the hair burned bright green with Kat's magic as the power soared through Rhys.

It felt like a dozen needles sinking deep into his flesh, like invasive threads tying into his veins, piercing his heart.

The pain sunk into his bones, and his body tightened up automatically, hands into fists, tendons rising in his forearms and in his neck as he gritted his teeth and rode through the discomfort.

When it was over, he expelled a relieved breath.

"You think that was bad," Kat said, "if something happens to Emery—"

"I know how it feels to die, Kat," he said. "I am undead, after all." He turned in his seat to Dane. "Call in the House."

"How many vampires you want?"

Rhys opened his car door and stepped out. "I want all of them."

CHAPTER 33

EMERY

Aunt Nina produced a blade from a sheath attached to her belt.

Emery's chin wobbled as tears burned in her eyes.

This was *really* happening.

Her *former* aunt, a witch, was seriously going to hurt her in order to kill a bunch of vampires.

How the hell had this become her life?

Heat ran through Emery, driving away the chill she'd been feeling since she woke in the dark, dank space.

That must have been the flush of fear.

"I'm no Redheart witch," Aunt Nina said. "But I can try to keep the pain at bay, all right darling?"

The fear was quickly burning to anger. "Fuck you."

Nina frowned as she stepped up to the table. She flipped a lever on the table's arm beneath Emery's wrist.

Emery flinched at the clang of metal. The cool blade came to her wrist.

Oh god.

Emery wiggled on the table, yanking on the straps, fighting with everything she had.

"It'll hurt worse if I'm trying to hit a moving target," Aunt Nina said.

Emery went still. Maybe if it was a clean cut, she could survive it...

The tip of the blade pierced her skin, and white-hot pain raced through her arm and across her chest.

Emery screamed and writhed trying to yank her arm away from the pain.

But it was no use. The straps were too tight.

She could only lie there and take it.

Aunt Nina stepped back, and Emery breathed heavily through the bright ache in her flesh and the ache that flashed in her vision.

The murmur of the witches grew more intense as Nina made her way around the table to the other wrist.

Emery lulled her head to her arm to see blood gushing from the wound and filling up a narrow trough in the table's arm. The blood ran down to a hole where it funneled to the floor.

The hell?

Nina stopped at Emery's other wrist, the blade poised to cut.

"It'll be over soon, darling," she said right before she plunged the blade into Emery's flesh.

The intense pain returned, and Emery squeezed her eyes shut and screamed at the ceiling.

She just wanted it to stop. She wanted it to be over. She wanted to go back to her life before all of this when she was in the dark about the supernatural world, when the worst thing she had to worry about was dodging Tanner's thoughts. Back when life seemed horrible, but was far simpler than she ever gave it credit for.

She wanted her Twizzlers and her Yellowstone sweatshirt and her comfy leggings and her stupid reality TV shows.

But she couldn't go back.

She couldn't go back to the person she was then.

And maybe...maybe she didn't want to.

Life was simpler back then because she kept her mouth shut and did what she was told. She made herself small and took on everyone's shit, both out loud and in their heads. She gave people what they wanted, sometimes before they even asked for it.

But she was tired. So fucking tired of giving up everything she had in order to keep things peaceful for the sake of peace.

She was so fucking done with allowing everyone around her to treat her like shit.

She was a demon, wasn't she?

And if she was a demon, then she had her own power.

She just needed to figure out how to use it.

As the blood drained from the slits on her wrist, Emery shivered and grew cold. Her head went swimmy, her vision teetering.

If she didn't do something soon, she'd be too late.

But as she lay there trying to think of what to do, a collective gasp went through the witches.

Emery lifted her head to see a ghostly figure standing in the middle of the room.

The woman was in a gauzy white dress that fluttered on a phantom breeze. And she was *floating*.

Had Emery died already? Was this some kind of angel,

come to carry her off? And if so, why could she still feel pain?

The ghost turned her head, and Emery caught sight of her white eyes.

"Oracle," Aunt Nina said, "you better be here to bring us good news."

The ghost spoke, her voice echoing around the room. "Death will come for some of you tonight."

And then the air crackled, and the ghost was gone.

"No," Nina said. "No!" She turned her head toward the vaulted ceiling. "Ciri! This isn't the deal we made!"

Somewhere, a door clanked open. Air rushed into the room.

It took Emery a second to realize that no, that wasn't air...that was just the speed of a vampire entering the room.

And not just one, but several.

With Rhys at the lead.

Somehow the cavernous space seemed to shrink in size around him. His eyes glowed predator blue in the dimness, fangs sharp as he spoke.

"It's time you witches burned," he said and then he lunged.

CHAPTER 34

RHYS

Rhys drank back the blood of a Ravenwood witch.

He drank her back and felt the thrum of her heart grow weak, then stop altogether.

The fresh sustenance hit his stomach and shot straight through his system.

The witch was dying, and he was fucking alive with her death.

The beat of the blood roared through his veins, pouring heat and strength into him.

They would not stop him.

They could not stop him.

He tossed the nameless witch aside and bit into the next.

Screams rent through the room as his Turned massacred those who'd done him wrong.

And then the floor cracked open, and one of his vampires tumbled through it, landing with a loud thud at the bottom of the cavern below.

The sound of a dozen bones breaking was an unmistakable sound.

"Stop," a woman said, her arms raised over her head. "Or I'll bring down this entire building."

Rhys dropped the witch he had in his arms. Her heart was still beating, but she was lacking in blood and close to death.

"What is your name?" Rhys asked the woman.

"Nina," she answered. "Wood."

"Ravenwood, you mean," Kat corrected.

"If you want to get technical," Nina answered.

Rhys stalked closer to the table where Emery's eyes were growing heavy. Rhys could feel their connection thrumming, but the spell didn't seem to be pushing his life force to Emery.

She wasn't healing.

In fact, she looked like she was dying.

"What do you want, Ms. Ravenwood," Rhys said. He tried to focus on the witch and not Emery.

Because if he let himself linger on her pale form much longer, there was no telling what he'd do.

He wasn't mad yet. He needed to think with a cool head.

"I want what you want," Nina answered. "To end the curse."

"Is that so?" Rhys came around the table. "Then let us take Emery and be done with this."

"She can't go, and you know that. She has to die."

He did know. But he was trying hard to ignore that fact.

There had to be another way, one they'd figure out together. They just needed to get out of here alive first.

"Why would you want to end the curse now?" Rhys asked.

When he got around the table, Nina took a step back,

keeping distance between them. He knew there was blood smeared across his face. He knew his eyes were still glowing blue in the dim light.

He was a monster, and he would do the dirty work to get the job done.

The witch was smart to keep her distance.

"We don't want to risk exposure," Nina said. "You and your vampires can't be losing control. Not in the twenty-first century."

"And Last Vale?"

Nina licked her lips. "I'm sure that's something we can negotiate later."

"You want access to more power," Rhys said as he continued to advance on her, "when you've kept a demon descendant in the dark for centuries, when you have Emery strapped to a table, the life draining out of her."

"As if you're innocent." Nina kept her arms raised, ready to strike if she needed to. "You're a vampire. You kill to survive."

"*My mom*," Emery mumbled.

Rhys glanced at her over his shoulder. Big mistake. He choked back a growl of fear as his throat went thick with worry. She was so pale, dark circles darkening beneath her eyes. The air was thick with the sweet scent of her blood.

"She...killed...my mom," Emery said.

Rhys looked back at Nina. "The girl is delirious."

"And..." Emery sucked in a breath that stuttered down her throat, "she wants...to...kill...you."

Rhys cocked his head and regarded the witch with new interest. "Is that true?"

Nina shook her head and took another step back. Rhys realized too late that she'd been making her way for a stone staircase. And as soon as she was up on the first step, she swung her arms down.

The floor spiderwebbed, and the stone crumbled beneath him.

Suddenly, he was falling through dark air, the rest of his Turned and Kat falling after him.

CHAPTER 35

EMERY

Emery was falling, and when she hit the bottom of whatever hole she'd fallen into, the air gasped out of her as the tell-tale sound of bones breaking reached her ears.

Pain was everywhere, in every hollow of her body, and she couldn't breathe, and she couldn't see straight, and...was she dying?

How much more could she take?

She gasped into the darkness.

Someone help me. Please.

The agony racing through her body was the kind of agony Emery hadn't thought existed.

She wanted to die.

She wanted it to stop.

She couldn't move for fear of more pain, but yet her current position made her ribcage burn.

"I've got you," Rhys said, his voice thick and winded as he appeared over her. He brought his wrist to his mouth and bit into his flesh. "Here. Drink."

"Wait," Kat gasped in the distance. "The spell...you can't—"

"She's dying, Kat," Rhys said over his shoulder.

"If...you...give her...blood...you might not...survive. It's too much."

"I don't care," he said with a growl.

Emery tried pushing him away when he brought his wrist to her mouth, but she had nothing left to give. No energy in her body, barely any air in her lungs. She could hear the slowing beat of her heart in her own ears, and she could have sworn her vision was starting to pulse with white light as if...

Was she dying?

When Rhys's blood hit her tongue, it was like a kaleidoscope hit her senses.

Red and blue and gold light flared in her vision as her veins went fizzy and hot. A buzzy warmth flooded her limbs, and her head lulled back, her eyelids growing heavy.

Was she floating?

She wanted to sink into the delicious warmth, the euphoria.

"Emery?" Rhys's voice came to her like a silk ribbon sliding over her skin.

"Huh?"

"Are you all right?"

She smiled up at him. "I feel divine."

The pain was gone. She could breathe again.

Oh gods, the relief of it.

Rhys tucked a lock of hair behind her ear, his fingers lingering on her skin. "I'm glad," he said.

"I think we have another problem," Dane said. He pointed up at the mouth of the cave-in where several figures had assembled, voices joining in a chant.

Emery blinked, clearing some of the tears from her eyes. The voices were so pretty. Like a lullaby.

"That's probably not good, I'm assuming?" Dane said.

"What do you think they're up to?" another vampire said.

"Improvising," Kat choked out.

Rhys held Emery closer. He was so solid, and she felt safe in the circle of his arms. She wanted to curl into him.

"What the fuck does that mean?" he asked.

"They were in the middle of a spell when we came in." Dane helped Kat up. She groaned once she was on her feet. "I'm guessing something to do with the curse."

"Let me heal you," Dane said to her.

"Vampire blood will muddy my magic. I can't risk that right now."

"If you've got broken bones and internal bleeding, you won't be able to do magic anyway," he pointed out.

"Focus," Rhys said.

"They were draining Emery's blood when we came in," Kat said, "which is now splattered all over this cavern."

The fizz of Rhys's blood was starting to wear off, but the pain was definitely gone. Even the slits on Emery's wrists had healed.

Apparently, vampire blood could perform miracles.

"They said they wanted to kill Rhys," Emery reminded them.

Rhys looked down at her, and the sharp scowl that had been permanently on his face relaxed a little. "You're looking better already."

"I feel better."

He turned back to Kat. "Could they kill me outright with Emery's blood?"

Kat leaned up against the cavern wall, her arm held tight

to her side. "The curse could still be in the blood, and we're literally standing over a ley line. Anything is possible."

"What would you do in this scenario?" Dane asked.

Kat winced with pain and held her breath for a second before answering. "Okay, so demon magic affects the mind. Ravenwood magic is elemental. Emery's blood holds the curse..." She trailed off, her gaze distant.

The air grew muggy. Emery could literally feel the humidity on her arms. Which was an odd thing, considering they were below ground, surrounded by rock.

The chanting grew louder.

"I'm just going to vault myself up there and start snapping necks," Dane said, but as soon as he bent, poised to jump, a rock the size of Emery's head flew at him. He crashed back, the rock at his sternum, and slammed into the cavern's wall.

"Fucking hell," Rhys said.

"I don't think we're getting out of this cavern just yet," another vampire said. Emery thought his name might be Cole, but she couldn't remember for sure.

"Come on, Kat." Rhys's voice vibrated through his chest as he spoke. If they weren't all under attack by witches, Emery would snuggle into him just to hear the deep rumble of his voice against her ear. "I need something to work with. Anything."

"I know. I'm thinking."

Cole swayed next to Kat. He shook his head like he was trying to fend off exhaustion. "Hey...um...guys. I don't feel so good."

Another vampire went down on her knees.

Rhys stood up and pulled Emery behind him using his body like a shield.

"What is this?" he said with a growl.

"I don't know. It's…" Kat smacked her lips together, and then she ran her hand up her arm. "The air is humid."

"I noticed."

Emery peeked over the rise of Rhys's shoulder. She could literally see the steam coming off the nearby rocks.

Kate's eyes got wide. "They're burning off Emery's blood so it turns into steam."

Another vampire put his hand out to catch himself on the cavern's wall.

"Making the curse—" Rhys started.

"Airborne," Kat finished.

CHAPTER 36

RHYS

Rhys could feel the wetness to the air, and now that Emery was behind him and not tucked beneath his chin, he realized he could taste her. The scintillating sweetness was on the tip of his tongue and quickly coating the back of his throat.

"Shit," Kat said beneath her breath.

The predatory burn went straight to Rhys's eyes, and in the cavern's dimness, the pulsing heartbeats came into stark relief.

Kat was across the cavern, Emery behind him.

There was a voice screaming in his head not to give in to the lust, but the voice quickly faded as the thirst took over, as it burned on the roof of his mouth.

The sharp points of his fangs grazed his bottom lip as the steady beat of Emery's heart filled his ears.

He turned, his veins suddenly burning for her, craving her.

There was only the pulsing ache in his throat and the thrumming beat of her heart.

Everything else disappeared.

"Rhys," she said.

That voice, like a breath on his skin.

He wanted to possess her. He wanted to drain her. He wanted to taste the final beat of her heart on his tongue.

He would have her. She was his. His to take.

"Rhys!" she yelled, her fear practically alive in the air.

The sharp tang of it, mixed with the blood, made an intoxicating blend.

He was the son of a mad king.

And he could fight the madness no more.

He lunged.

CHAPTER 37

EMERY

TRYING TO JUMP OUT OF THE PATH OF A CHARGING VAMPIRE was impossible, so Emery didn't even try.

But everyone kept telling her she had demon blood running through her veins, and she'd been fighting that, fighting accepting it, pushing the truth down deep no matter how much sense it made.

But she couldn't keep doing that.

She couldn't continue to pretend to be something she wasn't and hide everything about who she was.

She had a power no one else had.

The power to get inside a mind.

But how the hell was she supposed to use it on a vampire that had gone completely insane?

Her entire life, she'd kept herself quiet, never used her voice.

She'd been afraid of speaking up, afraid of how people would react, but worse, what they would think.

She'd fought her abilities her entire life and never used them to her advantage.

But that had been fear, too. Because for centuries, the Ravenwood witches had kept the identity from her and her family, kept them bound, kept them quiet and small.

Emery was not going to play that game anymore.

She was not going to be their tool to wield.

Adrenaline surged through her body. She balled her hands into fists at her side as Rhys came for her.

Gritting her teeth, Emery narrowed her eyes at him and said, "Stop!"

Something bloomed in Emery's chest. A rightness. A steadiness. The hair at the nape of her neck rose as goose-bumps went up and down her arms.

Rhys froze in place, his eyes glowing blue in the darkness.

The other vampires, gone to the lust, went still.

Kat was still against the cavern's wall breathing through her own pain. "Are you doing this?" she said. "Because I don't think I have much magic to give."

"I...I..." Emery was going to say, *I think so*, but that was the old her, the *small* her. "Yes," she answered. "Yes, it is."

"The little demon has found her magic," Kat said, the admiration bright in her voice.

"I don't know what to do now." The bloom in her chest pulsed like a living thing. She was distantly aware that the tattoo at her chest—the demon mark—was growing warmer, glowing red.

If the necklace had been a binding agent for her magic, it was now fully open to her.

She just needed to figure out how to wield it.

"You can do this, Em," Kat said. "You're already doing it."

None of the vampires moved an inch. They didn't even blink.

The witches above chanted faster, louder.

Now it was a game of tug-of-war. Who was stronger?

"When you hear someone's thoughts..." Kat paused to suck in a breath and then groaned as she repositioned herself. "What does it feel like when you hear someone's thoughts?"

"I don't know. I never thought about it, I guess."

"Well think about it now."

Rhys flinched and took a step.

Shit, she was losing her grip on him already!

Okay, think.

When she heard someone's thoughts, it was almost... almost like she was opening a door. But her entire life, she'd let the thoughts come to her.

Maybe instead, she needed to push the other way.

Emery inhaled deeply, filling her lungs, and then she squared her shoulders and gritted her teeth and pulled on that bloom in her chest.

She pushed out.

The tattoo glowed brighter.

Rhys took another step.

Emery put up a hand. "I am not your enemy, and I am not your meal."

Rhys blinked again. Emery pushed harder, sweat beading along her forehead.

"You need to fight it Rhys. Push through the hunger. You can fight it—I'll help you. You are better than this. Better than them. You will not give in."

Tension appeared in the faint creases around his eyes.

Emery pushed harder, imagining her own power

breaking the hold of the curse. It was no longer tethered to Last Vale, and it was no longer anchored to Emery.

It was losing its power, burning off like rain on a hot summer day.

"Come on, Rhys," Emery said. "*Fight it.*"

CHAPTER 38

RHYS

Rhys could feel the curse's hold on him, but it was growing weaker.

Emery.

Emery.

Her name was like a mantra in his head now as he felt the soft touch of her mind on the fringe of his blood lust.

He blinked.

You are not the blood lust, came her voice in his head.

Was he just imaging it? Or was she really there? Was she trying to pull him from the brink? From the madness?

I know you are better than this.

He wanted to believe her.

He wanted to believe in himself.

He'd always fought who he was, and who he thought he was destined to become.

But maybe he'd had it all wrong.

Maybe fighting it was useless. Maybe what he'd really

needed was to accept who he was and find a way to exist exactly as he was meant to be.

He needed a light to his darkness.

He needed Emery.

Her brightness warmed his cold heart. Her faith in him burnished his dark edges.

The curse's hold on him diminished.

Emery smiled at him. "Rhys! Rhys? Yes! Come back to me. Please."

He blinked several times.

Just keep pushing, she said. *I know you can break through this.*

The last tether of the curse snapped, and Rhys expelled a long breath like a man who had broken through the surface of a lake.

He rushed over to Emery. She squeaked and darted back, so he held up his hands. "It's all right. I'm me again."

She relaxed and allowed him to pull her into an embrace.

The scent of her blood was still heavy in the air, but there was something better, something more primal.

The scent of her, her skin, her hair, her very being.

He drank her in, the heady licorice scent of her, the softness of her body and the thread of her relief.

"Thank you," he said.

"It was nothing," she said, and then, "No, actually. It was awesome. I'm awesome. And you're welcome."

"Guys," Kat muttered.

Rhys turned to find his vampires coming out of the curse's thrall.

"Witches gonna run," Kat said.

The chanting had stopped. Footsteps shuffled above.

In unison, Rhys and his Turned tilted their heads up.

"Bring me my aunt Nina," Emery said behind him.

He gave her a nod of his head. "The rest are going to die."

And then he leapt from the cavern, his Turned not far behind.

CHAPTER 39

EMERY

It was Dane and Cole that helped Emery and Kat get out of the caved in cavern.

Once they were on solid ground, Dane gave Kat some of his blood. It was odd seeing someone else give in to that drunkenness.

Did Emery look that goofy as Rhys's blood coursed through her body?

Within seconds, Kat dropped her arm from her midsection and wiggled out her arms like she was shaking off a hard workout.

"That's much better," she said.

"I'm always happy to help." Dane winked at her.

"Where's Rhys?" Emery asked. "And my aunt and cousin?"

"Which one is your cousin?" Cole asked.

Emery held up her hand to indicate Beth's height. "A little smaller than me, dark hair."

"Ahh yes. Had a taste of that one. Reminded me of pond scum."

Emery couldn't help it—she laughed out loud.

"Come on, little demon," Dane said. "This way."

DANE AND COLE led them down a hallway where old scones in the stone walls glowed a soft golden light. Emery wasn't sure what this building was, or even where they were, but Kat had mentioned a ley line, and Emery automatically assumed that meant they were near Last Vale.

She couldn't wait to explore more of the ghost town. The history, the artifacts! So much to discover.

As they walked, Kat slung her arm over Emery's shoulder. "You did well."

The compliment warmed Emery from her head to her toes. She didn't know much about Kat, but she definitely knew Kat was way cooler than she was and had far more experience.

"Thank you. That means a lot."

"Once this BS is behind us," Kat said, "I'd be happy to help you navigate your powers."

"I'll take all the help I can get."

Dane cut left into an open doorway.

They walked into a large room with high ceilings and a bank of windows along the far wall. The ocean glowed silver with moonlight outside the windows.

Tied to chairs, Aunt Nina and Beth sat in the middle of the room with two vampires flanking them and Rhys directly behind them.

Blood ran from a cut on Beth's forehead and more from an open bite wound in her neck.

There was a bruise turning bright purple on Aunt Nina's face, but no obvious teeth marks from what Emery could see.

A flash of sympathy ran through her, only for her to quickly squash it when she reminded herself who these women were, and what they'd done to Emery and her mother.

They made a bridge collapse beneath Mom's car and sent her sailing down a ravine.

Emery could still remember sitting at home, wondering where her mom was, and why she was so late coming home.

And afterward, Aunt Nina had doted on Emery while cooing, "There, there, you poor thing. I'm so sorry."

Aunt Nina had killed Mom and kept Emery like a prisoner.

All because of a grudge several centuries old.

All because of a battle over land that supposedly held great power.

Mom shouldn't have died over that.

No one should have.

Dane leaned against the edge of an old wooden desk and crossed his arms over his chest. "What do you plan to do with them, little demon? With that newfound power of yours, maybe you can make them believe they're pigs and send them out to roll in the mud."

Cole snickered. Rhys sent a withering look Dane's way.

Dane just shrugged.

Emery didn't want to fight anymore. She didn't want to torture others. And she didn't want to humiliate them even though they'd kept her family prisoner for a very long time.

She wanted them to go through what she'd gone through.

"Are there any Ravenwood witches left besides these

two?" she asked.

"They've met their demise," Rhys reported, his gaze dark.

"Good," Emery said as she paced in front of her aunt and cousin.

Beth sneered at her. "I'm not afraid of you. You're nothing. I'm a witch. A Ravenwood. Whatever you got, it isn't as powerful as what I have."

"Oh?"

Emery stopped in front of her cousin and bent over, her hands on her knees, putting her gaze level with Beth's eyes. "You're so proud of your heritage? Your witch blood?"

"Of course I am," Beth said.

"How about I make you forget it?"

Finally, real fear washed into Beth's expression. Her mouth gaped open. "No. Emery. Come on. You can't be serious—"

"Oh I'm very serious. You and your mom knew what I was. You knew and you kept it from me, and instead, you treated me like I was beneath you. How about we turn the tables?"

Emery wasn't sure if she could deliver on that promise, but she was sure as hell going to try.

She reached for that now familiar bloom at her chest and opened the figurative door.

Power rushed through her, and though she didn't look down, she could see the tattoo—the demon mark—glowing in her periphery vision.

"Emery!" Beth said. "Don't—"

In the past, Emery had only gotten surface level thoughts from Beth, and now she realized it was because Beth knew to shield her mind from Emery to a certain degree.

Let's just see her shield this.

Emery pushed out.

She knew the second she was in because Beth's face went blank.

Beside her, Nina was yelling something, but Emery didn't hear her. She was solely focused on Beth, on the shadows of her mind.

That honeyed warmth flooded her body as she pulled on that magic.

Forget you are a witch. Forget everything you know about being a witch, she thought. *You're just a loser who can't hold down a job, who has nothing going for them. You are beneath me. In fact, you're beneath everyone.*

When Emery released her, Beth jolted upright, her eyes big and her mouth hanging open. She blinked several times, tears escaping her, and then looked up at Emery. "Cuz?" she said. "What's going on?"

"Get her home," Emery said to no one in particular.

Rhys snapped his fingers, and Cole jumped into action. "Come on, loser," he said to Beth. "Time to go back home."

Emery turned her attention to Aunt Nina. Tears streaked through Nina's makeup. Mascara was smudged beneath her eyes.

"Emery," she said, "you don't have to do this."

"Oh? And when I begged you to stop just, what, an hour ago? Did you?"

"Emery—"

"Did you?!" Emery shouted.

Nina flinched. "I'm sorry, dear. I really am. We were trying to save the city and stop the curse and—"

Emery didn't let her finish. She pulled on her power. And as the demon mark pulsed brightly, Emery pushed into Nina's mind and wiped it clean.

CHAPTER 40

EMERY

"Good morning, little demon," Dane said.

Emery looked away from the coffee pot to frown at the vampire. "Will you stop with that? And it's four in the afternoon."

"It's morning for me."

He was standing in front of the closed windows behind him. The sun was still shining outside, but in House Roman, it was hard to tell. Not a rogue ray of light was allowed to penetrate.

Emery was still getting used to shifting her schedule. She didn't want to sleep all day, but she didn't want to miss being with Rhys either.

For now, she went to bed around five a.m. and got up around one. It suited her well considering she no longer worked for TS Jenison.

When she'd told Tanner she was quitting, he pretended like it was no big thing while inside he freaked the hell out. *I can't lose Em. She literally knows everything. I don't even know how to log into the company's C drive. Shit. Fuck. What the fuck am I going to do? Keep her. You gotta keep her, man.*

"How about if I promote you?" he said. "Make you executive assistant?"

"I already am, Tanner."

He gave her a face like he was totally shocked by this news. "Sorry, I meant, Chief Administrative Officer."

"What's the pay?"

His expression went blank again while his thoughts were very clear.

Shit, I don't know what her current pay is.

"Thank you for offering, Tanner," Emery said, "but I already accepted a new job working for Rhys Roman."

"You what?!"

"His offer was one I couldn't refuse."

"That motherfucker. What is he paying you? I'll double it."

"Nice try, but you can't afford me, and I doubt you could match his benefits package." Then she smiled deviously to herself, grabbed her already-packed bag from her desk, and exited that office like she was fucking Queen of the City.

Of course, the benefits package came with a very sexy vampire in her bed, and sex that couldn't be matched.

And a house in Second District.

And, yes, even a job.

Rhys had asked her to oversee the revitalization of Last Vale. They were several years out from its unveiling since they had a lot of spin to put on the situation, considering the town already existed and no one knew about it.

But damn if she wasn't looking forward to the task.

She couldn't wait to get her hands dirty.

"Out," a deep, gravelly voice said.

Emery had been dying for a fresh cup of coffee, but the sound of Rhys Roman giving a command was just the same as a jolt of caffeine to her veins.

When she turned away from the coffee maker, Dane was already gone. And a blink later, Rhys was standing in front of her, caging her against the counter.

"Hello, little lamb," he said.

"Hello, old man," she said.

He grumbled, and the sound reverberated through his chest as he pressed closer.

With Dane, she hated the cute names. With Rhys, it turned her fucking wild with need.

Rhys's gaze sunk to her throat. "I'm thirsty," he said with a growl.

"Oh? I made coffee."

"I don't want coffee." His hard cock dug into her thigh. His hands went to her ass, and he quickly hauled her up onto the counter, spreading her legs so he could press in between them.

"I think there's juice in the fridge," she said as she slowly tugged down the hem of his black pajama pants.

"Not that either." His nose went to her throat as he inhaled deeply.

Emery shivered as her body tried to curl into itself as Rhys's exhale tickled the sensitive flesh just below her pulse point.

Rhys kissed her, then dragged his teeth over her flesh.

Good god.

She freed his cock and wrapped her hand around him. The head of his shaft throbbed in her grip. "Water then?" she said.

"I want to taste what's mine," he said at her ear.

"And what's that?"

With his hands still on her ass, he yanked her to the edge of the counter.

"You." Then he sunk his teeth into her throat.

EPILOGUE

Ciri entered the warehouse on the edge of the ocean, on the edge of Last Vale.

She could still smell the demon blood in the air.

Good.

With magic still shielding the town on all sides, Rhys Roman had no reason to lock the doors, and so Ciri entered the warehouse without any effort at all.

Night had fallen, and the air was dark. Rain pattered against the roof and dripped from the end of Ciri's nose.

It was the perfect night for what she needed to do.

Ciri went down the hallway and entered the cavernous storage room. The floor was gone, leaving a dark pit at its center.

After assessing the damage, she found a way down on the edge of the room, using large pieces of stone like steps to get to the bottom.

Magic pulsed in the air.

The ley line was strong here, and some of the girl's blood was still waiting in the crooks and crevices.

It had been so long since Ciri had been able to work her special brand of magic.

It had been so long since she'd acted as the traveler she was.

She waved her hands through the air.

The ley line pulsed through her, like an unseen river, unstoppable, a force to be reckoned with.

For hundreds of years, she'd been unable to open a gateway to Alius.

She'd been trying to heal the break, treating it as if it were a crack that just needed mending when instead she should have been looking at it like a fire that needed kindling.

Her own oracles came from Alius, and it was through an oracle that she'd been given the information she'd needed. A little demon blood was all it took. It was so simple, so obvious, and she chastised herself for not figuring it out earlier.

Then again, everything happened when it was supposed to happen.

The mortal world was breaking, spoiling at its core. Some of it was the fault of the mortals themselves, and some of it was orchestrated.

Regardless of the origin, the world had grown ravenous. Social media and politics and the internet. It was like an ouroboros, like a snake eating its own tail.

Something needed to change. It had to change before it devoured itself. Before they were all turned to dust.

Ciri waved her hand through the air, and the dried demon blood turned wet again and beaded on the rocks. Ciri's chest heaved as the power raced through her, as the air became charged and electric.

It was working. It was finally working.

Excitement danced along her skin and churned in her gut.

The air cracked open, and bright light glinted out.

Yes!

She pushed out with her hands, pushing more power into the crack.

Come on.

The air tore wider, and a shadowy figure appeared on the other side.

Just a bit more.

Ciri gritted her teeth, planted her feet on the stone floor.

So close now.

Light shone across the cavern like a supernova. Ciri squinted her eyes against it. If she pulled her arms away now, the power might crash, and who knew if she could get it going again? It'd been centuries since she'd gotten this far.

The cavern glittered bright like stars.

The hair lifted on the nape of Ciri's neck.

Come on. Come on.

With one final push, the air cracked and a gate arched out in a half circle.

And the Demon King stepped through.

THE DEMON KING **has started a new monarchy in the United States.**

Nothing can stop him. Nothing can kill him.

Now there are websites dedicated to worshipping him. Countless internet memes about how ridiculously gorgeous he is. And yeah, I can admit he's fine as hell. But he's a villain to end all villains. There's no way I'm falling prey to that.

That is until I accidentally cross paths with the Demon King. Wrath demands I bow to him. For a second, I almost do. Being around him is...*consuming*. But dying is better than surrendering and I refuse.

Except when Wrath turns his dark, dangerous power on me...it doesn't work.

And now the villain is looking at me like I'm the enemy.

~

Order Ruthless Demon King now so you don't miss out!
https://geni.us/ruthlessdemonking

~

WANT A STEAMY BONUS SCENE FROM RHYS'S POINT OF VIEW?
Download here: https://geni.us/rhysbonus

ALSO BY NIKKI ST. CROWE

Wrath & Rain Trilogy

Ruthless Demon King

Sinful Demon King

Vengeful Demon King

Vicious Lost Boys

The Never King

The Dark One

Their Vicious Darling

Cursed Vampires

A Dark Vampire Curse

Kindle Vella Serial

Hot Vampire Next Door

ABOUT THE AUTHOR

Nikki St. Crowe has been writing for as long as she can remember. Her first book, written in the 4th grade, was about a magical mansion full of treasure. While she still loves writing about magic, she's ditched the treasure for something better: villains, monsters, and anti-heroes, and the women who make them wild.

These days, when Nikki isn't writing or daydreaming about villains, she can either be found on the beach or at home with her husband and daughter.

Exclusive Member's Only Access
https://www.subscribepage.com/nikkistcrowe

Gain early access to cover reveals and sneak peeks on Nikki's Patreon:
https://www.patreon.com/nikkistcrowe

Visit Nikki on the web at:
www.nikkistcrowe.com

tiktok.com/@nikkistcrowe

instagram.com/nikkistcrowe

facebook.com/authornikkistcrowe

amazon.com/author/nikkistcrowe

bookbub.com/profile/nikki-st-crowe